First Kiss
by
Bernadette Marie

5 Prince Publishing, Denver, CO

This is a fictional work. The names, characters, incidents, places, and locations are solely the concepts and products of the author's imagination or are used to create a fictitious story and should not be construed as real.

5 PRINCE PUBLISHING AND BOOKS, LLC
PO Box 16507
Denver, CO 80216
www.5PrinceBooks.com

ISBN 13: 978-1-63112-024-4 ISBN 10: 1631120247
First Kiss
Bernadette Marie
Copyright Bernadette Marie 2012
Published by 5 Prince Publishing

Author Photo: Damon Kappel/Studio 16 2009

Second Edition/Second Printing February 2014 Printed U.S.A.

5 PRINCE PUBLISHING AND BOOKS, LLC.

For Stan
I'm glad you were my last first kiss.

Acknowledgements

Stan, thank you for making this my reality by letting me spend all day doing what I love. T, N, G, S, and J you all amaze me with you love and support. You are all so creative and I can't wait to see what you do with it. Mom, Dad, and Sissy thank you for you love and support of all the crazy things I do.

Viola thank you for taking my half-ideas and making them fabulous! Connie and Marie, thank you for keeping my life organized. Anne, thank you for your wisdom of words and their order. Amanda and Gloria, thank you for jumping in and throwing yourself on this project!

To each and every one of my readers who give me reason everyday to write the stories that fill my brain, I appreciate your love and support. There is nothing I enjoy more than bringing you new heros and heroines to love.

Bernadette Marie

Dear Reader,

Welcome to Aspen Creek, Colorado. This small mountain town has many stories and Cade Carter and Olivia Baker's story is just the first to be shared in my newest series Aspen Creek.

Cade Carter lived with his single father in this small town. He grew up next to Olivia Baker and his cousin Conner Carter, and this was where their story began.

But as every story of childhood friends, people grow up, move away, and become who they will become for life. However, sometimes those paths cross again, even if fate is engineered.

Please join me in Aspen Creek and meet all the inhabitants of this quaint little town, both currently and those who laid the foundation for the town generations ago.

Happy Reading
Bernadette Marie

Chapter One

There was a chill in the air, even in June. Cade Carter rolled the windows up on his Porsche as he began his decent into the valley. The mountains of Colorado could deliver any unprepared traveler an array of weather to cope with, and it could change without warning in a matter of moments.

Though the higher peaks still boasted snow, he'd found the entire, long and boring trip from Green Bay, Wisconsin, to be fairly dry. Cade had considered driving his Bronco to Aspen Creek, but he'd needed the speed of the sports car and Ashley had needed it to move.

He glanced at his Rolex for the sixth time in the past half hour. He was going to be late.

Who was he kidding. He'd had no intentions of getting to his own father's funeral on time. Had it not been for Ashley, he'd have blown it off all together. But no. The words still rang in his ears. "You have to go. He was your father. He loved you. *You owe him…*"

Cade gripped the steering wheel tighter. He did owe him the decency to be at his funeral, because Cade Carter had been the worst son, and he knew it.

The first sign that would alert drivers to the small town of Aspen Creek was coming up on his right. A left would take him over the next hill to the elite ski resort town of Aspen Hills. The road he veered down would drop him into small town hell.

As the deep groves of Aspen trees thinned he could see the small town at the bottom of the valley. Each street was visible, the cars looked small, and the town stood there as if someone had taken a picture of it fifty years earlier, not one thing had changed. He did see a 7-11 sign peeking above the buildings. Corporate America had moved in. That was new. At least he'd know what the coffee tasted like.

He could see City Park in the center of town. The grass was green. Green's Market had the most cars in the parking lot and Sloan's Diner must have just finished with their lunch crowd.

Aspen Creek rolled along the sides of town and under the Rose Bridge. It was fast, unforgiving, and cold all year long. He'd had his share of dunks in that water, some on purpose, some not. Beyond the bridge and the white rapids of the river that rushed through town with its new melt off he could see the street where he'd grown up, where his father had lived, and where he'd fallen in love as a young boy.

Cade pulled the car to the shoulder of the narrow road and slammed it into park. He lifted his sunglasses from his eyes and rubbed them. He hadn't been back to Aspen Creek in twelve years. Long had been forgotten the sentiments of home, like people knowing your name, and not because you were some famous football player, but because you were Austin Carter's son. High school football games, swimming in Aspen Creek, and the girl next door were things a man forgot about when he was an M.V.P.

He blew out a long, ragged breath. The comforts of a sports car were limited to the power of the engine on a man Cade's size. He tried to stretch his legs, but to no avail. If he didn't get out and walk around soon he'd be paralyzed in the car seat. Just another thing he deserved he supposed. Career killing injuries were just another daily reminder that he was lucky to be alive, even if he now stood on the sidelines and basked in the glory of what used to be.

It was easy for the team to cut him loose when he was no longer able to perform. The position needed to be filled by someone younger and able to play. He was just a washed up has-been now who'd collected his payout.

Adjusting his sunglasses back on his face, he put the car back into drive. He had demons to face and he'd better just get it over with. Ashley was housesitting in Green Bay and Cade was expected back in three days. He couldn't imagine closing out his father's life could take longer than that.

Olivia Baker sat in the cemetery alone, next to the new grave and sobbed. The funeral had been small, but Austin had kept to himself for the past two years. She wasn't sure everyone had even heard he'd passed. She wiped her eyes. No, they all knew he'd died. He'd died right in her arms and that had gotten the attention of the local gossips.

The casket had been lowered, the chairs had been collected, and now the only man she'd ever cherished lay beneath the mound of red Colorado soil with a spray of wilting flowers atop it. It didn't seem dignified enough.

Her jaw clenched when she looked at the few bouquets and sprays that still lingered near the grave. Not one of them had Cade's name on it.

Damn him anyway.

What kind of son didn't even make it to the funeral of the man who raised him? The kind like Cade Carter.

The arrogant, self-centered bastard probably had some pressing football engagement and couldn't be bothered with his father's passing. Some dry-cleaners probably needed him to cut their big obnoxious grand-opening ribbon with an oversized pair of scissors, and to Cade that would have always been more important than respecting his father.

Olivia noticed she'd twisted the head off a carnation at her fingertips. She unclasped her hands and looked beyond the new grave to the one next to it.

CONNER CARTER.

Looking at the name written in stone sent chills up her spine. She looked away. She wondered if anyone at all had come to that funeral. She hadn't. She'd been tucked away safely in Grand Junction, again, when Conner had died. She was sure Austin had paid to bury him and had splurged for the headstone too. And she couldn't help but wonder if guilt over Conner's death had in some way contributed to Austin's death.

Just beyond the gate to the cemetery she could hear the sound of tires on the gravel. It didn't phase her. Neither did her responsibilities at the bank. Her boss Parker Woods had told her to take her time and that was what she was doing. She was in no condition to head back to town and act professional.

Tears streaked down her face from under her dark sunglasses, and she let them fall.

The hole in her heart from Austin's absence ached and she wondered if she'd get over her loss. Her son Gage would never remember the man she adored and loved. He'd never know how much Austin Carter cherished him and loved him.

Olivia squeezed her eyes shut tight. Would she miss Austin everyday when she looked into Gage's eyes and saw the resemblance?

She wiped away the tears and then noticed that the driver of the car, which had parked in the lot had walked across the gravel and stood only a few feet from her. She did what she could to compose herself. After all, she owed it to Austin to be gracious and welcoming to his mourners.

Olivia pushed herself up from the ground, brushed off her black skirt, and turned toward the person standing behind her.

There was an uneasiness that settled in Cade's gut when he saw the mound of dirt before him. Could guilt kill a man of his stature?

The woman who had been sitting at his father's grave stood before him, her elegant black dress covered in dust, but she didn't seem to mind.

He swallowed hard. "Is this Austin Carter's grave?"

The woman shook her head more in an effort to convey disgust than to signal that he was in the wrong place. "Why did you even bother?"

"I beg your pardon."

"Why show up now, Cade? You couldn't even give him the decency of being here on time?"

"I…" he had no answers. Besides who was she to be criticizing him?

Cade examined the lean, yet curvy woman in the well-worn dress who stood before him. Her hair was pulled back and dark glasses covered her eyes. Little gold bands adorned each of her ring fingers, so she could have been someone's wife. Hell, he'd grown up in the town, maybe he did know her. But still, what he did to get the funeral on time, or not, was not her concern.

"I guess you know me. Who might you be?"

The woman opened her mouth, and then shut it again. Instead of answering she picked her purse up off the ground and searched inside. She pulled out a business card and handed it to him. "I'm the one in charge of closing out your father's estate."

With that, she started off to the parking lot and he watched. Back in town five minutes and he was already pissing off the women there.

He ran his hand over the back of his neck and looked at the card as the woman sped away down the hill toward town.

Olivia Baker, Vice President Aspen Creek Bank.

His head shot back up and the air in his lungs escaped him.

A man could drive into town, and the girl next door, whom he'd fallen in love with as a child, could hand him a card with her name on it and he didn't even recognize her.

Suddenly the aches and pains in his leg, from his brush with death, didn't hurt as bad when he was faced with a woman scorned and a week in small town hell.

Chapter Two

Olivia pulled open the bottom drawer of her desk and threw her purse inside. Its contents spilled.

She'd clean it up later she decided as she kicked the drawer shut.

"Everything okay?" Parker Woods stood in the doorway to her office.

"Just fine." She fell into her chair and nearly missed the edge, sending it and her back into the wall. She gripped the armrests and steadied herself.

Olivia sucked in a deep breath of stale office air and tried to calm down before she passed out in the warm office in front of Parker.

He took a step further into the office. "The service was nice. You did a fine job with the arrangements."

She nodded slowly. "Thanks."

The air in the room only grew thicker the longer Parker stood there. She didn't want to kick her boss out, but if he didn't leave, she was going to have to make him and, with the mood she was in, it was going to come out wrong.

Parker shoved his hands into the pockets of his suit pants and rocked back on his heels. "You know, if you're not comfortable having to work with Austin's family on closing out his estate, I could handle it for you."

"I'm sure Cade and I will be able to handle things just fine."

He nodded slowly. "Kat said she passed a red Porsche in town with Wisconsin plates."

Ah, small town gossip at its finest. Kat McCormick could dish it with the best of them. Did the ex-home economics teacher turned bank teller not learn from years in high school that rumors and gossip were vicious weapons? But Olivia knew what was going through the minds of everyone. Had Olivia been having an affair with Austin Carter? And when his son, her ex-best friend from childhood and town bully, returned, what would he think of it?

It was reasons such as that which had sent her to college in Grand Junction for six years. She'd tried to make it last forever. But Aspen Creek would always call her back.

"I gave Cade my card and told him I was in charge of the estate. I expect to see him shortly." She picked up a file on her desk and began to look it over. "He'll want to get back to his lavish lifestyle as quickly as possible, I'd imagine."

Parker's eyes had grown wide. "You saw him then? He actually showed?"

Olivia dropped the folder back to the desk. "Showed? An hour and a half late to his own father's funeral is not what I call making an effort to pay your respects."

"Maybe something happened."

She cocked her head to the side. "He happened, Parker. He's never going to change. This town, his father, his cousin…" Her throat closed and she forced herself to breathe. "He moved on from here. None of us were good enough to be part of Cade Carter's life. The memory of Austin Carter will be better served if I give Cade a pen and the papers he needs to close everything out and let him get out of town as fast as he can."

Parker bit down on his lip and nodded again. "Offer still stands if you want me to take care of it."

"Thank you. I'll be fine."

He turned to leave and stopped just short of crossing over the threshold. With his back to her he spoke softly, "I'm sorry again for your loss."

Then he was gone.

The tears were back, but she didn't want to cry. Enough tears had been shed, and she knew these tears weren't for Austin. They were for his son.

He hadn't even recognized her.

In all fairness, it had been twelve years. Everyone changed in twelve years, and she'd changed more than most. She wore her hair shorter now, just grazing above her shoulders. When he'd seen her last, it had hung low down her back and curtained her face. There were no more thick glasses, poor posture, and layers upon layers of clothes to hide her body, which was now sixty pounds lighter. There was no reason for him to have recognized her at all. But she'd hoped that the young boy she'd loved was still buried inside the man somewhere and he'd have known her. But those days had passed when Olivia moved away from the house next door to Austin and Cade Carter, the day her step-father drug her away from the only people who ever cared for her.

She picked the file back up and turned toward her computer. No need to cry over a friendship that was lost at the age of twelve. No matter what a man promised you when he was a boy, it was no longer valid when he was a man.

Cade tucked himself back into his small car. He wasn't sure what he thought he'd find when he arrived at the cemetery. Maybe he thought he'd find nothing and no one. He had planned to be late enough to pay his respects privately and escape. The last thing he thought he'd find was Olivia Baker crying over his father's grave. He drove away from the cemetery. Hundreds of people had been laid to rest there from movie stars to John Does. He wondered which one he would be.

The road curved back down into town and the "Welcome to Aspen Creek" sign stood prominent at the entrance. Below it was a growing list of notables who had once called Aspen Creek their home.

Lillian Rose had grown up in that town and gone on to be a Hollywood icon of the golden picture era. Rose Bridge bore the name of her family. The ranch on the hill, overlooking both Aspen Creek and Aspen Hills, still had a Rose decedent living there.

Hunter Galloway was an author. Cade remembered having to read one of his books in school. Maybe that was something he should do again. They'd named the town library after him, so maybe he was a good writer.

Celeste Kirby was a gold medalist in figure skating. He'd actually known her, he thought back, but he couldn't really remember any details.

The last plaque that had been added to the sign was Home of Cade Carter. M.V.P. Superbowl XX—the rest of the Roman numerals had chipped away.

Cade let out a snort. They'd honored him with cheap paint. Well, it was indicative of his career.

The play he'd been credited with, which had earned him that M.V.P. title, was the play that had nearly killed him. His shoulder cramped, and when he straightened it, a pain shot through him all the way down to his leg. There was no need for fancy signs to make him remember what he'd had. He had plenty of pain, everyday, to remind him of that.

He passed by Sloan's Diner. The old, green Ford pickup was still parked on the side of the building. Mr. Sloan had had that truck for a million years. Cade smiled as he rolled through the stop sign at the corner. He'd eaten more meals in that diner than he had at his own kitchen table back in Green Bay.

Green Bay. That reminded him. He'd better call Ashley. His stay was certainly going to take a few more days than he'd expected.

He drove down Main Street, slow and easy. The pace hadn't changed. With that noted, he remembered why he'd left. He needed people and fast pace to survive. He could feel his own life slipping away as he drove through town.

The bank was up ahead. He could just stop, take care of everything he needed to, and head back home. Then he thought better of it because that would mean having to face Olivia. The one thing he'd never forget about Olivia Baker was her temper. The very thought made him laugh aloud. He tilted his head so he could see his reflection in the review mirror. Above the rim of his glasses, he could still see the scar that ran through his eyebrow. Yeah, she'd made forever marks on him in more ways than one.

No, he'd save facing Olivia for another day. He sped up and cleared through the rest of town as he headed for Rose Bridge. As he crossed it, his fingers tensed on the steering wheel. Twelve years was a long time to stay away from home, and the closer he drove to it, the more anxious he became.

It was just a house. No one lived there anymore. He took a deep breath. God, this trip was going to kill him.

Cade pulled up in front of the house where he'd always lived… until the day he'd driven away forever. The large oak in the front yard shaded the driveway, which was in need of repair. He pulled into the drive, put the car in park, but didn't turn the engine off. He'd never felt so alone in all his life.

The grass looked as if it hadn't been watered in years. The paint was peeling from the house and the porch swing hung from only one chain. The large detached garage at the back of the driveway had a broken window in the door.

He let out a long sigh. He'd have to hire someone to fix this dump up before he could sell it.

Was this his father's idea of getting back at him for abandoning him?

Cade turned off the car and slowly climbed out. He stood there, grasping the door and the roof of the car until feeling came back to his leg, and then he slammed the door and limped toward the porch.

An eerie wind blew through the trees and Cade stopped again. He glanced to his right and took in the sight of the small house next door. It had been Olivia's house once, but unlike his, she'd never called it a home.

The window, which overlooked his father's driveway, had been her bedroom. It faced his bedroom window. How many nights had they talked into the wee hours of morning from behind the screens? They'd made a million plans between the ages of six and twelve. Some were well thought out summer days with a picnic near the river, while others were conjured up ways on how they could run away from home. Olivia was usually the one wanting to run, and Conner was quick to get in on those plans. How ironic that she and Conner had returned to Aspen Creek, and he'd run.

His attention shifted to the tree in the back yard. He couldn't help but smile when he noticed the pieces of their tree house still lodged among the branches and the tire swing swaying in the breeze.

It was the building that tree house that gave him the scar over his eye. Olivia sucked at swinging a hammer, but if he remembered right, Conner fared worse. She'd nearly driven a nail through Conner's hand. He'd cried like a baby and bled a lot. Olivia turned from builder to nurse. She'd bandaged his hand and kissed his cheek. Even so many years later, Cade could feel the sting of jealousy burn through him.

He shifted his stare from the tree house to the lot behind his father's back yard.

He slowly walked through the back yard to the edge of the property and stood almost frozen in his footsteps.

The property which extended into the hillside belonged to his father. Out of his generosity, he'd built a house there among the groves of Aspen trees for his sister and her son.

Conner had lived there most of his life, just feet from Cade, but they'd never lived the same kind of life. In hindsight, Cade had had a beautiful childhood, even without a mother. But Conner, well, his life had always been hell.

Now, as the breeze blew around him, he looked beyond the trees to where the house had stood. Only the burned out shell remained. Conner had died there. That much he knew.

He forced himself to look away. The midday heat was getting to him. He needed to go inside and get a drink of water. Then he would assess what needed to be done and figure out whom to hire to take care of it.

Cade Carter didn't belong in Aspen Creek anymore. He felt that deep in his bones.

He walked back to the front of the house and pulled out the key he'd shoved in his pocket before he'd left Green Bay. Chances were his father had never changed the locks.

But as he lifted the key to the lock, the door pushed open under the slight weight of his hand. Well, that made sense too. It was Aspen Creek. Who was going to break in here?

Cade stepped into the house and shut the door behind him. It was dark and musty. His father must have holed up there for months.

Immediately he noticed the television stand was empty, and there was a dust-free space where the TV had sat. He cringed. He knew exactly who had been there. Surely, his aunt had helped herself to anything important. He'd have to ask Olivia if his aunt had been there for the funeral. Perhaps that had been the opportune time to clean the house out while everyone else was mourning. He wouldn't put it past the witch.

As he moved through the house, it grew darker where the drapes were closed. He hit the light switch, but nothing happened. Great, the power had been turned off. Slowly he started up the steps, each one harder than the last. When he reached the landing, he turned toward his bedroom and paused outside the door with his hand on the handle. He should have been back there. What kind of son completely forgets the father that loved him?

He turned the knob and pushed open the door.

For a moment, he just stood there looking in. Not one thing had moved from its place in twelve years. All of his trophies and medals were right where he'd left them. The posters still hung to the wall, and his running shoes were still tucked under the bed. Either his father had closed him off too, or he'd kept it the way it was in case he came back.

Cade walked into the room. It wasn't hard to pick up on the fact that someone had been there—recently. Every trophy had been dusted and the carpet had been vacuumed.

Did his father know he'd be home?

Had he set it up for him to return?

Or had he spent all of his time there?

Cade felt the air in his lungs grow thick. He left the room and shut the door behind him. His father's room was next to his and it too looked the same, though the bed was rumpled. But it was the next room that caught his eye. There was a twin bed by the window, fully made with throw pillows and a quilt at the foot, and a dresser he didn't recognize sat against the wall. But the object that had caught his attention was a crib in the corner of the room.

That had never been there. Cade felt his palms start to sweat. What was his father doing with a nursery set up in his house?

The June heat was closing in on him just as the house was. He needed that glass of water.

He hurried down the stairs as quickly as his stiff joints would let him and straight to the kitchen, but he stopped as he crossed the threshold and held his chest. His father had died in that room. He felt it. Cade closed his eyes and took a deep breath. He too had had his brush with death. He never wanted to feel that feeling again.

Pushing past his feelings, he opened the cupboard, pulled out a glass, and turned on the faucet. No water.

"Damn it." He set the glass down on the counter. Well, he wouldn't be staying there.

Again, he looked around the kitchen and into the other room. He'd have to stay in town and work on getting the utilities back up and running. Then he'd have to formulate a plan to clean the house up. No one would buy it the way it was. This certainly wasn't what he expected when Ashley had forced him to head to his father's funeral.

He headed to the front door, but something caught his eye under the couch. He bent down slowly and picked up the little car. It had been Conner's. The unsettled feeling of death washed over him again. Cade looked up the stairs toward the room with the crib. Toys and cribs—someone had been staying with his father. Still an uneasy feeling kept with him. Whose baby had been staying there, playing with childhood toys? What had his father been up to since Cade had left him twelve years ago?

Olivia turned off her computer and gathered her purse from her desk drawer, picking up the contents that had spilled out earlier. She'd expected Cade to follow her into town, but the familiar pang of disappointment, which usually accompanied any thought she'd had of Cade over the years, was all she'd gotten.

Parker walked through her office door. His tie had been loosened and he carried his suit jacket over his arm. She loved that he took his job seriously enough, even in the small town, to still dress like a big city bank president. That was some of the allure when he'd offered her the job. Parker Woods was a considerate and kind man.

"I'll walk out with you," he offered.

"Thanks." She walked to the door, turned off the light, and followed Parker out of the bank as the security guard locked the door from the inside and waved.

Parker dug his keys from his pocket. "Any plans tonight?"

"No. Not much in the mood to do anything but fall into bed."

He gave her a slow, thoughtful nod. "I'm really sorry about Austin. He was a good man."

"Thank you. He was a good man." She unlocked her car door and opened it. Austin had been gone nearly a week, and it hurt every day to know she wouldn't be stopping by to see him after work.

"I was wondering if you and Gage had a free night this week." He stepped toward her. "I have my kids, and I thought we could all go get a pizza."

Olivia didn't want to even think about making plans. She didn't want to get too cozy with Parker Woods. Mixing business with pleasure always spelled disaster. However, when she grew tired of mourning Austin's death, Parker might be the perfect distraction—but not yet.

"I'm still unpacking. Can I give it some thought?"

Parker stepped back. "That's fine." He unlocked his car and opened the door. "Hey, if you need any help getting settled into the new house, let me know."

"Thanks."

Olivia climbed into her car and shut the door. Parker waved as he drove away, but she sat quietly, her keys still in her hand.

Her new house was a fresh start. When she bought it, she hadn't thought she'd be so lonely. Guilt plagued her. Austin had lent her the money, and when she tried to make plans to pay him back, he wouldn't hear of it.

"It's for you and my Gage. Take care of him."

She didn't know a month later…well, that it would all be over.

Tears stung her eyes again, and she wiped them away. She should have seen it. She should have known Austin was up to something. Olivia and Gage had been perfectly happy living with him when they'd moved back from Grand Junction after Gage was born. She'd ignored the idle rumors that they were having some inappropriate affair and just was happy for once.

Gage gave Austin such pleasure. It shocked her the day he mentioned she should get a place—then he gave her the money.

"Cade has his own money now. He doesn't need what I've saved. Conner is gone. You're the only one who's ever taken care of me. You deserve it."

His words lodged in her chest.

He'd known his last days were coming, but that was a secret he'd kept from her. Emotions stirred in her that she didn't know what to do with. She loved that crazy, old man, but he shouldn't have done what he did.

Well, she'd get the money back to the rightful owner. She'd just have to pay Cade.

Olivia started the car and backed out of the space. Maybe she could talk to Parker about a loan from the bank. If she could just pay Cade off in one lump sum, she'd never have to see him again.

She was sure that was what he would want.

If she knew anything about Cade Carter, it was that he hated the fact he had to come back to Aspen Creek and he was making plans again to escape as quickly as he could.

Chapter Three

It was dreary when Olivia pried her eyes open the next morning. Rain softly pelted the roof with its rhythm and the sun's rays had not yet made it through the clouds.

Gage had been up all night with night terrors, and she'd slept, again, in the chair next to his crib.

She didn't know why he had them, but people told her he'd grow out of it. They'd had this same routine for almost eighteen months, and she was beginning to wonder.

Now that it was time to get up, he was resting peacefully.

Olivia pulled the light blanket over his sleeping body and rested her hand on his head. She'd never expected to become a mother, but it was the greatest gift anyone had ever given her. She'd protect her son with her life if she had too, and she'd love him enough for two parents.

She brewed a pot of coffee and quickly took her shower before Gage woke. She readied him, and they headed into town to start their Friday morning.

Gage quickly fell into place at the daycare center as Miss Michelle carried him off, and he waved goodbye to Olivia. She, on the other hand, was not feeling as ecstatic about her day.

As she started her car, she contemplated her finances. The daycare bill wasn't due for another week so she could splurge on a gourmet cup of coffee and a muffin at Molly's. Maybe that would make this pathetic morning sunnier, even if just emotionally.

She parked the car, pulled out her umbrella and headed toward the small building that had once been the original location of the bank.

"Tell me they make decent coffee here." The voice rang out from behind her.

She turned to find Cade standing only inches from her.

His hair was wet, and he wore his sunglasses on the back of his neck. She'd been so angry with him yesterday she hadn't taken a moment to realize what an enormous man he was. Perhaps that was because his shoulders had been hunched and his tail was between his legs. But now he towered over her, and even though he didn't play football anymore, she could tell he obviously still trained.

His biceps pushed the limits of the T-shirt he wore, which was wet and clinging to his sculpted chest.

Olivia cleared her throat and her mind. "Best you'll find on this side of the mountain."

He chuckled at that. "Well, Aspen Hills probably just charges more."

Was he trying to be easy with her? He obviously knew who she was now. She let out a slow breath. She didn't want to be nice to him. That old friendship didn't belong there anymore. Now he was the man she owed, and she didn't like that either. But when he smiled and it sparkled in his eyes, she was twelve again.

Cade reached around her and opened the door. "It's drier inside."

She hesitated for a moment then started inside and closed her umbrella.

The bakery wasn't as busy as usual. Most people, like her, were probably taking their time getting into town.

Molly Fields stood behind the counter with her infectious smile. "Mornin', Olivia. What can I do for ya?"

"I'd love a mocha and a cran-orange muffin."

"Comin' up," she said as she looked past her toward Cade. "And for your friend?"

Cade smiled and held his hand out to her. "It's Cade, Cade Carter, Mrs. Fields. It's nice to see you again."

"Oh, my!" She looked him over and then slid a glance toward Olivia.

Olivia felt herself tense. She'd thought more of Mrs. Fields than to make quick judgments, but she knew that was what she was doing.

Mrs. Fields patted Cade's hand. "I'm sorry to hear about your daddy. He was an upstanding member of this community. We're all going to miss him."

"Thank you." Cade retracted his hand and even stepped back from the counter just a bit.

"So, what can I get for you?"

"You know, I'll take what she's having."

Mrs. Fields walked away to gather their order.

Cade moved in closer behind her. "I don't think she likes me."

She didn't look over her shoulder to look at him. "You were late to your own father's funeral. No one saw you there. In this town, that's a sin."

"C'mon, at least I'm here."

Olivia swallowed hard. "For the first time in twelve years and he's dead, Cade."

"Point made," he said as he stepped back again.

Mrs. Fields set their coffees and muffins on the counter and rang it into the cash register.

Olivia reached into her purse for her wallet.

Cade stepped up to the counter. "I've got it."

He pulled the bills from his pocket and set them on the counter. Olivia picked up the purchase and headed out the door with her umbrella tucked under her arm.

The rain had increased, but she didn't care. She just wanted to get in the car and drive away.

He was following her as quickly as he could. From the corner of her eye she could see that he limped, obviously residual effects from his accident. If she just hurried, he'd never catch up with her.

But he called out to her, "Olivia, what's gotten into you?"

She hesitated at the car. "I have to get to work."

He moved quickly as she opened her door and blocked it before she could get in. The water dripped from her hair into her eyes, and she tried to bat it away.

"Hey, I know you think I'm just some asshole who never called his father, but I thought we were friends."

"We were friends. When we were little. You didn't even know who I was yesterday." It hurt when she said it. Why should she care?

He raised his eyebrows. "You have to admit you look a bit different."

"I never should have become unfamiliar to you." That hurt the moment she said it so she just went on. "You can't actually expect me to stand here and feel sorry for you, do you? Your daddy died and you're doing your duty to come back here. You never cared, Cade. You only cared about yourself." She pushed past him. "He was proud of you. He loved you. Your silence hurt him."

"And you know all of this because you stayed in this hell hole and never got out? Because he got them to paint my name on the sign outside of town? Proud of me? He cared more about you and Conner than he ever did about me."

If her hand had been free, she'd have slapped him across the face, but instead she climbed in the car and slammed the door.

She set the coffee in the holder, started the car, and backed out of the space narrowly missing him. Perhaps if she'd tried harder she could have run him over, but, then again, he'd probably only end up denting her car and that would cost her too much to fix.

The bank was only two minutes away. She wondered how she was going to compose herself in those two minutes.

She was officially late when she walked into the bank. It had taken her four passes through town to calm down enough to walk through the door and straight into her office where she threw the full cup of coffee and uneaten muffin into the trash.

Kat was quick. She was at the door the moment Olivia slid out of her jacket.

"You doing okay? Thought maybe something was wrong. You're never late"

"Nothing is wrong, Mrs. McCormick. I'm just late."

"Oh, how many times do I have to tell you that I'm not your teacher anymore, and you can call me Kat." Olivia nodded. Kat moved to her desk and rested her hands on it. "Heard Cade Carter made it to town after the funeral."

"You heard correctly."

"Have you seen him? My daughter said she heard he'd stayed in town last night at the motel."

"The utilities were turned off the day after Austin died. As per his request. I think he didn't want his sister to move in."

"Ugly woman." Kat shook her head. "Abused that little boy of hers something awful and just abandoned him to Austin for months at a time. Shame too, he was a smart cookie. He could have gone places."

"He did. He was a Marine."

"That's right. I did hear that. Got caught in some crossfire when al-Qaeda took out some town full of women and children."

Olivia felt the chill of sweat bead up on the back of her neck. She'd heard the story, in vivid detail, and it still made her sick.

She nodded toward Kat and sat down in her chair.

Parker tapped on the door. "Everything okay?"

Olivia blew out a breath. Why did everyone feel the need to coddle her? "Everything is fine."

"You have a visitor." Olivia stood from her chair and Parker moved in. "It's Cade."

Her breath caught, and Kat's lips formed a grin that had gossip written all over it.

She leaned in closer to Olivia. "You should head to the restroom and fix yourself up. The rain got you good."

Kat turned to leave, and Parker stepped up to her desk. "Want me to take him? I'm sure he's here on Austin's behalf."

"No, I'll take care of it. Just stall him a moment and let me get cleaned up."

Olivia hurried out of her office before Cade saw her and headed to the restroom.

When she returned, he was seated in one of the chairs in front of her desk. His sunglasses were still on the back of his neck and his shirt was still damp from the rain.

She shut the door behind her, and he turned.

"Thought maybe Parker led you out the back door."

"I'd considered it."

He let out a chuckle as she sat down behind her desk.

"I didn't remember Mindy's bakery being so good," he commented.

"She has a good little business."

"You know, I'm sure Kat would have snatched up that coffee and muffin you threw in the trash. She always was a sucker for a baked good."

Olivia's stomach twisted. She looked in the trash next to her desk and prominently displayed on the top was the full cup of coffee, now leaking into the can, and the uneaten muffin.

"I'm sorry. I'd lost my appetite. I'll pay you back."

"I'd settle for you just to talk to me like I didn't run over your dog."

Olivia sat back in her seat. "This has been a hard week. Having you here seems to be making it harder."

He leaned in closer to the desk and rested his folded arms atop it. "Is that because you didn't expect me at all?"

"Cade…"

"No, I don't blame you. Why would anyone expect more?" He sat back in his chair. "So you said you were in charge of things. What does that mean?"

Olivia dropped her shoulders and did her best to not be so uptight. After all, it wasn't her father that had died, it was Cade's. Even if he hadn't been around, she needed to respect that he was the one who had lost his father. "Austin had some accounts and a safety deposit box."

"Great, tell me what to sign and I'll get out of here." His voice was anxious Olivia narrowed her eyes on him at his comments.

"Wouldn't want to keep you." She snipped at him. "I'll need the power of attorney papers as well as his death certificate."

His eyes shot open wide. "Shit! I don't have any of that." He came forward on his chair and rested his arms on the desk again.

"Cade, you can't close out anything without them or attempt to sell the house. They should have been in the mail." She laced her fingers together and dropped them on her desk as well.

"Dad's mail? There's no mail in his box."

Olivia fisted her hands. She'd made arrangements for him to have those papers. There was no reason he should be seated before her without them.

Cade tapped his fingers on her desk. "Where do I get them?"

"You'll have to contact the county and have them sent to you."

"Great. What will that take? Six weeks?" He was perturbed, and she found humor in it. He fell back in his chair again.

"If you're lucky," she added, knowing she could tell him that he could drive to the county seat and probably get it in his hand. She'd also pay a call to the postmaster to find out where Austin's mail had been forwarded. But she wasn't going to share anything with Cade so she sat calmly. It was better to watch him stew.

He focused his eyes on her, and she felt her palms begin to sweat. He leaned in even closer over the desk.

"Who arranged his services?"

"I did."

"Who turned the water off in his house?"

"I did. I can have that turned back on…"

"Did it." He clenched his jaw. "Did you take the TV?"

"What? No."

He nodded as if he'd known that was going to be her answer. "If you arranged his service and took care of his house, wouldn't you have gotten those papers? Seems you were pretty close to the old man."

Olivia straightened her spine. "I took care of him, Cade. The man died in my arms in the kitchen." The anger and hate that she'd bottled up over Cade Carter was fresh and raw now. She struggled to keep her calm. "I made sure he had three square meals a day. I made him take his medicine, and I drove him to Gunnison to see the heart specialist that was recommended. He treated me like a daughter, and he respected me, and that is a lot more than I can say for any other person in this town."

She took a deep breath, aware that her voice was rising.

"The paperwork should have been mailed to his house. But now you'll need to get that paperwork to me before I can help you, Cade."

He gave her another nod. "My aunt...did she come to the funeral?"

Olivia shook her head. "I thought someone said she'd come to town, but I didn't see her, and I would have. It was a small crowd." And that bothered her. Austin had closed himself away from the world. He should have had the whole town there, so why wasn't the world mourning as much as she was?

Cade ran his tongue over his teeth and took in the sight of her sitting so professionally behind her desk. He'd thought of her over the years, but, of course, the image he had of her didn't fit the woman before him.

Her chocolate brown eyes were soft, and today her brown hair fell over her shoulders. The black suit she wore made her look smart, but he already knew she was. Maybe it was fate he'd returned and had to do business with her.

He looked over her interlaced fingers resting on her desk. Each ring finger had a dainty gold band. He wasn't sure if that was a symbol or a fashion. It was time to find out who Olivia Baker was now. It would give him something to do while in Aspen Creek, and it looked like he'd be staying awhile.

Cade crossed his arms over his chest. "So did you ever get out of this hell hole?" He asked realizing it was the worst way to put the question. "Probably didn't get to college like you'd wanted to, did you?"

Where had he lost his art of conversation?

Olivia held her chin high. "I went to Mesa University in Grand Junction. I graduated with a 3.8. I have a degree in finance." She locked eyes with him. "Yes, I got away."

He swallowed hard. "It did good for you, even if you didn't leave the state. You look real good." His compliment didn't even sound like one, and she shook her head. He was in too deep now, which meant he couldn't stop talking. "So what brought you back?" He tried to gain back some composure, but suddenly any social skills he had seemed to be flying out the window.

"I came back to take care of your dad when I found out he was sick. And I got a really good job offer. We returned to this *hell hole,*" she used her fingers to emphasize his quotation, "about a year and a half ago. We just bought the old Alistair place over on Elm." She smiled when she said it.

"Yeah, I know the place. Hung with Patrick Alistair in high school. Though I think he was a senior when we were freshmen, but he could get beer." God, he was sounding so juvenile. It pained him to hear his own voice. "So, you said we?"

"I beg your pardon?" Her beautifully sculpted eyebrows had drawn together.

"You said *we.*"

A different smile formed on her lips. "Oh, yes, I did. Gage and I."

Gage. The name stuck him in the chest like a knife because he'd seen the spark in her eyes when she'd said his name. "Lucky man."

"I hope he thinks so." She stood from behind her desk and looked down at him. "Well, Mr. Carter, I assume I'll see you again when you have the appropriate paperwork."

He realized his cue and stood to leave the office.

Olivia reached out and touched his arm. "Cade," her voice was hushed and the hardness of her eyes had softened. "I'm really sorry about your dad. I cared for him so much." The sincerity piqued his interest.

When he turned to her and met her eyes with his, he felt her hand tremble just as he felt his own knees go weak. Yeah, he thought, she felt it too. Damn it to hell, that Gage was a lucky guy.

He could find no words for her compassion. He slipped on his sunglasses and headed out of the bank.

As he walked out, he gave Kat McCormick a nod, and she smiled a crooked smile. Yeah, she'd have plenty to gossip about this summer. Olivia Baker, vice-president of the Aspen Creek bank, had just made him feel as little as he assumed he'd made her feel most her life, and he was sure it showed in his face. Well, it wasn't the first time either of them had been the fodder for town gossip, and he was sure it wouldn't be the last.

Chapter Four

Olivia walked through the door to the post office just before closing time.

"Cutting it pretty close, aren't you?" Clive, the postmaster, gave her a friendly smile.

"I know, but I just need some information."

"Well, then, I'm your guy. What can I help you with?"

Olivia pushed back her shoulders and sucked in a breath of courage. "I need to know where Austin Carter's mail is."

Clive's lips pursed, and he narrowed his eyes on her. "You know I can't give that information out."

"I assumed so, but nothing has been delivered to his house since he passed and we're expecting important documents."

Clive gave her a slow nod and leaned in over the counter. "I could tell you that you might want to talk to Ms. Carter."

"Austin's sister?"

"Just saying. Her name was still listed as a resident."

The woman was a vulture. Olivia gave him a warm smile. "I'll look into that." She turned to leave.

"His son is in town, isn't he?"

Olivia stopped and turned back. "For a few days."

"I'll stop by on my route and give my condolences. Mr. Carter was a fine man."

She gave him a wave and left. Yes, Austin Carter was a fine man and, at that very moment, she missed him terribly.

The water and electricity had been restored to the house, and Cade was happy to not have to stay in town another night. He would, however, need to find some clothes. He'd only brought enough for three days, and it was a little cooler in the valley than he'd thought it would be. Perhaps he'd head over the mountain to Aspen Hills and buy something better than what the local general store had. He cringed when he thought about it.

After his meeting with Olivia, he'd called Ashley, who was sitting poolside enjoying a beer—*his* pool, drinking *his* beer. The whole thought made him mad.

He was tense. That was all. This little town made him that way. Perhaps he'd head into town and throw a few back himself. It wasn't fair that Ashley was living it up in *his* house while he was obsessing over Olivia Baker and her absolute hatred of him and her very obvious affection for his father.

That clinched it. Perhaps a really good drunk would help him clear his mind, and maybe, just maybe, he could find out why Olivia was so attached to his old man and why there was a nursery upstairs.

There was only one problem with working at a bank, Olivia decided as she wiped the fog from the bathroom mirror…getting up before the sun on a Saturday morning to go into work. She couldn't really complain. They all took their turns. Today it was her and Kat. It just might make for a very long four hours.

Michelle knocked on the door just after seven as Olivia filled her travel mug with coffee.

"Gage is still asleep," she whispered as she let Michelle in the front door. Thank God for Michelle. Every other Saturday she'd worked Austin had watched him, up until she'd moved out of his house. Then he'd been busy. Only *now* she knew that had been his excuse since he was getting sicker.

"Did he have another bad night?"

"Yes. He's only eighteen months old. I can't image what he could possibly have terrors over."

"Did you have them when you were little?"

She thought about it. "I don't think so."

"How about his dad?"

Olivia shrugged her shoulders, not wanting to even think about his father. She turned and headed toward the kitchen. She pulled a mug from the cupboard and handed it to Michelle. "So, what are your plans?"

Michelle took the mug and filled it from the coffee pot on the counter. "I thought we'd head into town and play at the park for a little bit. My sister and niece were going to meet us there."

And it was reasons such as setting up play dates that made Michelle not only Gage's favorite teacher but her favorite sitter.

"Why don't I just plan to meet you in the park around twelve-fifteen."

"Sure."

Olivia was content with the arrangement. Gage was indeed a lucky man, she thought as she remembered Cade's words from the day before. He was lucky to have people who cared about him.

The town was still quiet when she drove down Main Street and headed toward the bank. Usually, she'd use her Saturdays at the bank to catch up on her work. Other than the few people who didn't make it to the bank on Friday with their paychecks or the ranchers who came in from beyond the city limits, there wasn't a lot of banking traffic.

Earl, the night guard, opened the door for her, and she'd almost made it in to her office before Kat burst through the door behind her, nearly knocking Earl over on her way.

"Oh, do I have something hot to tell."

Olivia closed her eyes and sucked in a breath. This was the only part of small town she didn't like. "What's that?"

"Cade Carter is in jail."

Olivia felt the blood drain from her face, and she forced herself to concentrate. "What? Why?"

"Guess he headed into town last night and got drunk. There were enough fans around for a bit to talk football, so he bought a few rounds. Then he threw Buck into the jukebox."

Olivia balled her fists at her side. "Was Buck hurt?"

"Oh, you know, he was so drunk he probably didn't feel a thing. Juke box won't play, and they had to call the cops."

This wasn't exactly how she thought Austin would have like Cade's homecoming. She pinched the bridge of her nose. She was going to need more coffee to get through her day.

"Did they press charges?"

"Nah. Owner said Buck had it coming. He'd challenged Cade on some football mishaps, told him he didn't deserve the M.V.P. for that play in the Super Bowl, and then he said something about Conner, and that was when Cade took the swing."

Olivia gritted her teeth. Even dead Conner could get Cade in trouble.

Kat started toward the break room to discard her personal items. When she returned, Olivia was still standing outside her office door.

Olivia tried to act casual, but she'd been so stunned by Kat's news she hadn't been able to get to work. "So what happens now, for Cade?"

"Oh, Sheriff is just letting him sleep it off. That gossip over at the 7-11 says he's got a huge black eye and a busted lip. Otherwise, he's fine. But he's going to be hurting today."

Olivia was grateful when the door opened, and a customer walked toward the counter.

She retreated to her office and shut the door. Perhaps she'd just lay her head on her desk and catch some sleep. She certainly wasn't going to be able to focus on much.

For the first time in the almost two years since Olivia had been back to Aspen Creek, the bank had been busier than she'd ever seen it on a Saturday. She helped Kat at the teller window, took four applications for ranch equipment loans, and had to open the vault for a safety deposit box for Mrs. Krane, who just wanted to see her husband's old wedding band, again. She missed him that much.

When they locked the door at noon, Olivia fell into the seat of her car and let out a long and ragged breath.

The night of no sleep, followed by the busy morning, and then the constant worry over Cade had completely exhausted her.

What bothered her even more was the fact that Cade wasn't hers to worry about, and he was taking up way too much of her time by doing so. But still, deep in her heart, he was her friend, and, above all else, he was Austin's son.

But as sons went, hers was much more important, and she was going to hurry to the park and pick him up from Michelle. Nothing would make her day better than wrapping her arms around him and holding on tight.

Gage had run to her the moment she climbed from her car. It was if he'd known she needed his undying love.

Michelle followed him. "He's been playing hard."

"Good, maybe he'll go down for a nap. Mommy sure could use one, too."

"You let me know if you could use some help this weekend finishing up the house or watching Gage so you can get some things done."

"I appreciate that." Olivia looked into her son's sleepy eyes. "I think, for now, we're going to go to the store and buy some macaroni and cheese."

Gage's squeal of approval was exactly what she'd needed to change her poor attitude.

Gage sang as Olivia pushed him through the store in the cart. She gathered her son and the few bags and headed out to the car. It had been busy enough that no one chose to corner her and discuss the events of the past few weeks. She wasn't keen on the way people looked at her and Gage, and then mentioned Austin as if she'd done something immoral by taking care of him.

Having buckled Gage in his seat, she opened the trunk of her car and began to load the few bags of items they purchased.

"You wouldn't give an old friend a lift, would you?"

Olivia spun around when she heard the deep, gruff voice behind her. Cade limped slowly toward her.

"Old friend, huh?"

The corner of his mouth turned up into that crooked grin that got him into more trouble as a kid. "I don't remember you being so hard to win over when we were little."

"I've done a lot of growing." She gripped her keys in her hand until they dug into her palm. "You don't have your car?"

"I was fairly sure I'd be better off walking last night. I left my car at home."

She wanted to laugh at how casually he called his father's house *home*. "Your eye looks bad." She reached to touch it, but quickly retracted her hand. What was she thinking?

He touched it with the tips of his fingers and winced. "I've had worse. But its sore enough I couldn't even put on my sunglasses."

Those blue eyes she'd once known so well gazed at her, and she didn't like that he could still make her melt.

He touched her arm. "So, what do you say? Gage won't get mad if you give me a ride, will he?"

At that moment, Gage let his opinion known by yelling "mac n cheeeeese" from the back seat. Olivia smiled, and Cade's eyes narrowed.

She closed the trunk and walked around the side of the car with Cade following close behind.

"Gage Baker, where did you get that?" She reached in the car and took the sucker her son was trying to get into his mouth.

His protest was cut short when he saw the man standing next to her. Gage covered his eyes and looked through his fingers.

Cade shook his head. "Gage? This is Gage?"

"Yes," her voice was soft. "Cade, this is my son, Gage."

He let out a chuckle and took a step back. "I thought you said your husband was Gage."

"No, what I said was Gage and I moved back to Aspen Creek and bought the Alistair house. The rest you decided on your own."

"And you didn't correct me."

Olivia shrugged. "I suppose we could give you a ride home."

Cade climbed into the car, and Olivia backed out of the parking space.

Cade turned his body to look at Gage who was singing a song with no understandable words. "I can't believe you're a mother."

"Why? Or is it more that you can't believe that someone would have found me appealing enough to…"

"What I mean is…" Well, he didn't know what he meant. But no matter what, it was sounding bad. "I don't know why. I guess I just never thought about it. But most of my friends are married and have kids. Half of them are divorced, and a few of the people we grew up with are already dead."

His own breath hitched when he said it, and he saw her stiffen.

Olivia pulled into the driveway and parked behind his Porsche. He didn't move right away. There was a comfort sitting in Olivia's car, a comfort he'd forgotten.

"Why don't you guys come in for a while?"

"I have eggs and milk in the back."

"I have a fridge," he said as he opened the door.

Gage piped up with, "In! In! In!"

Cade smiled. "You might be surprised to find out I make a mean mac and cheese."

He opened the back door to the car and began to unbuckle the toddler. Gage watched him carefully, but when his seatbelt was unfastened, his arms reached up. That did something to him. It tugged at his heart as nothing ever had. He looked at him. His eyes. They were familiar. Cade let out a breath and pulled the little boy from his seat. There was a connection—a familiarity.

By the time he'd come around the front of the car, Olivia was climbing out.

"Cade, I don't have time for this." Her voice was sharp.

"In!" Gage rested his head on Cade's shoulder, and it pierced him with a sincerity he'd never felt before.

"This is ridiculous." Olivia shut the door. "Now you have turned my son against me."

"No one is against you, Olivia."

"Hmm," she huffed as she walked to the back of the car to retrieve her groceries.

He watched her for a moment. She wasn't comfortable around him, but she once was. Then he realized the reaction to his statement was justified. Cade had turned against her once. He'd turned, and he'd justified everyone else who had turned their back on her. The only people who had always believed in Olivia Baker were his father and his cousin, and now they were both gone. No wonder she was gun shy. She was also mourning, and the combo could be quite dangerous.

He carried the toddler into the house and set him on the floor. Immediately Gage went for the couch and crouched down. He looked under the couch then around the side as if he were looking for something he knew should be there.

It occurred to Cade that Gage had been there before. This was the baby who'd been playing with the toys. That made sense now. Olivia would have had him there. His father would have known this child.

His heart ached. Did Gage understand that the man who'd lived there was gone?

"Are you looking for this?" Cade picked up the car he'd found under the couch and held it out to Gage.

Gage's eyes lit up and he hurried across the room to retrieve the car and then ran back to the coffee table and pushed it around.

Olivia opened the front door carrying a bag of groceries, and Cade hurried over to help her. "I'll put this in the fridge."

"Thank you."

He walked to the kitchen and pulled open the door to the refrigerator. "I don't have anything to offer you to drink. In fact, it looks like we will have to use your milk and butter to make lunch."

There was a scowl on her face when he mentioned it. He'd never thought about someone else's financial circumstances before. Perhaps his sharing in their meal was going to cost her. He'd make it up to her. Having her there, he realized he owed her that consideration and more.

"I have some juice in the car. I'll go get it." She left through the front door.

Gage looked up, watched her, and then went back to playing with his car. Cade thought it was interesting that he didn't run after her. Most kids would run if their mother left, but he was comfortable in the house. He was comfortable with him.

When Olivia walked back in the house, Gage only looked up. She smiled at him and went about finding everything she needed in the kitchen to make the juice.

Cade rested against the counter. "You're awfully comfy in this house."

"Spent a lot of time here in my life."

That was true. She never did want to be home when she lived next door. Even after she'd moved across town and when they weren't on speaking terms, she still came by to see his father and Conner.

"Gage seems comfortable here, too."

Olivia cast a loving glance at her son. "He's spent a lot of time here, too."

"Is that his crib upstairs?" he asked as if the connection finally made sense.

She casually nodded. "We stayed here when we moved. Your father offered, and then I could take care of him."

"So why move out?"

"He asked me to."

That was an interesting twist, Cade thought. He took a breath to ask her why he'd have pushed them out when Gage interrupted.

"Mickey."

They both turned their attention to him, and Olivia abandoned her juice making and walked into the other room.

She pointed to the stand where the TV had been. "The TV is gone. See."

"Gone."

"Yes. You play with your car, and then we will eat lunch. Then home for a nap, okay?"

Gage went back to playing as if his mother's explanation was enough for him, and she returned to the kitchen and pulled a pot out of the cupboard and filled it at the sink.

Cade moved in behind her, closely. "I said I'd make lunch." He took hold of the pot and Olivia quickly moved away from him, but not before her scent washed over him.

"I'll go get Gage ready."

She disappeared again, this time returning with a diaper bag and a few of Gage's other toys.

By the time Cade was finished making lunch, they were seated at the table with Gage on Olivia's lap. Cade dished out the macaroni and cheese, set it on the table, and then sat down with them.

There wasn't much talking between them. Olivia helped feed Gage, but Cade noticed she only took a few bites of her own lunch. When Gage was done eating, he turned around on his mother's lap, rested his head against her shoulder, and was fast asleep.

"He's a good boy," Cade said softly as not to wake him.

Olivia rubbed his back. "Yes, he is."

"Where is his daddy?"

Olivia stiffened and pushed her bowl away. "Gone." She wrapped her arms around her son and stood. "I should get him home."

Cade stood and reached for her. "Please don't hurry off. His crib is upstairs. Let him sleep."

"I don't think…"

"Don't think." He let his touch linger on her soft skin. "I'd like the company."

Olivia looked around. "You're going to have to sell this place, aren't you?"

"Yes."

Her eyes had softened. It probably broke her heart more than his to know the house would be sold. "I could stay for a little while and help you clean up. I know you're probably in a hurry to get back to Wisconsin."

She walked away and took Gage upstairs.

When Olivia made her way back into the kitchen, Cade was gone. She looked out the window and could see that he was in the garage.

She looked around the house. It was empty, not in belongings but in personality. Austin's spirit wasn't there; his laughter didn't fill the rooms; his love and compassion would be missed.

Tears stung her throat. His life was too short. How was she going to go on without him? How was Gage?

Perhaps it would be good for her to help clean up the house and get it ready to sell. Cade would be gone soon. Austin and Conner were already gone. It was time to say goodbye to the Carter house, too. This would give her closure.

She began airing out the house by opening the windows in the living room and kitchen. After looking down at her clothes, she decided it would be in her best interest to find something else to wear. She didn't have many business suits. Ruining one wasn't an option. More than once she had pulled an old T-shirt from Cade's closet. She'd do it again. He certainly couldn't fit them.

Olivia pushed open the door to Cade's room. Austin had always kept the room the way Cade had left it. She'd seen him go in there on occasion, but she didn't ask him why. Though, now that she was a mother, she understood needing a connection. Didn't she sometimes hold Gage's blanket to her cheek when she missed him, and he was only in the other room?

But the room was different now. The curtain was open and light filled the room, which was usually dark. The air was clear. She looked at the trophies and they had been dusted. If the entire house needed to be cleaned, why had Cade started in there? Or had it been cleaned before he arrived?

She went to the closet and pulled out one of Cade's old T-shirts, the ones he'd left when he decided they weren't worth his time—when he'd fled Aspen Creek.

She tore an O. U. shirt off the hanger. She quickly unbuttoned her blouse, slid it from her body, and pulled on the T-shirt. As she moved to leave, she noticed a few photographs lying on the dresser. They were pictures of her and Cade—one in the tree house, another on the first day of third grade. Why were they there? She let the memory of their friendship wash over her. Could they really start all over again?

Once she was back in the kitchen, she retrieved the dusting cloths she herself had stored under the sink and dusted the living room.

Gage had always slept through vacuuming so she vacuumed the room as well, and then checked on him. She wished he slept as well during the night. Then maybe she wouldn't be such an emotional wreck.

Cade, however, still hadn't come back into the house. Olivia walked out the front door, and there he was.

"You're fixing the swing?"

"Almost done." He looked up at her. "Nice shirt."

She looked down at herself. "I hope you don't mind."

"O.U. never looked so nice on anyone else."

Her heart kicked up a beat. "So, of all the rooms you've cleaned, why start with your bedroom?"

He looked up at her, his hand still securing the chain. "It was that way when I showed up. As if he knew I was coming and would need a place to stay."

She was sure of that now.

Olivia watched as he tightened the last bolt and gave the chain a solid tug. The muscles in his arms tightened. "That should do the trick."

Cautiously, he sat down and gave the swing a push.

Olivia watched as he lifted his hand to her, and she took it. She sat down next to him, and he draped his arm over the back of the swing and pushed them into motion with his foot.

"We used to spend a lot of time on this swing," he said casually.

"We sure did." She swallowed hard. "We made a lot of plans here."

Cade laughed. "Remember how Conner thought we could turn the tree house into a rocket ship?"

"If anyone could have made it happen, it would have been him."

He turned and studied her. "He was smart, wasn't he?"

"Smartest man I ever knew."

"Why do you suppose he failed out of school?"

Olivia shrugged her shoulders, uncomfortable with the subject. "It's hard to fight the kind of abuse he was dealing with."

Cade only nodded. She knew he didn't want to face the fact that that was exactly what was going on in Conner's life while Cade strived to be the best athlete and get every pretty girl in the back of his car.

His arm moved from the back of the swing and now rested on her shoulders. She tried not to tense, but she was sure he'd felt her do so. He moved his arm back to the swing. "How old were we the last time we sat here? Twelve?"

She sucked in a breath. "Eighteen."

Cade gave her a questioning glance, and she gripped her hands together and set them in her lap. "I had come over to see your dad. He wasn't home, and you were sitting here. You told me to sit and wait."

"Oh, yeah."

She wondered if he recalled it at all, really. She had been in her oversized clothes with her hair shielding her face and her thick glasses slipping down her. Did he remember that she sat on one side as tense as she was now while he smoked a cigarette, which his father would have hated?

Did he realize that he'd not said a word to her after she had sat down? Did he remember that a few minutes later Parker's sister had pulled up in front of the house and called her a nasty name, and that he'd laughed and then took off with Patsy as they both laughed?

Olivia turned and looked at him, and, at that moment, she knew he'd remembered it. The look of terror on his face as he looked back at her said it all.

She rose to her feet. "I should go."

He reached for her. "Olivia, I am so sorry."

She took a step back from him. "Cade, this isn't important. I just need to go."

"I don't want you to run from me. I'm not who I was back then."

"Really? Because I would have thought you would have been here then."

She stepped around him and headed up to get Gage. Only five minutes later, with a crying toddler, she was driving away.

Chapter Five

Olivia set Gage on the floor with his toys and turned on the TV. She started his movie and headed back out to the car to retrieve her groceries.

As soon as she'd opened the trunk, she realized she'd left some of them at Cade's house. With a string of curses, she slammed down the trunk door. She wasn't going back. She had just enough money she could replace them, and she was going to avoid Cade Carter the rest of the time he was in Aspen Creek. She was already a wreck with Austin gone and Parker asking her to dinner. The last thing she needed was Cade slipping his arm over her shoulders and promising her he'd changed.

It was getting dark, and a soft breeze blew the curtains in a lazy wave. Olivia decided it was time for dinner. They had a routine and that brought her an immense amount of joy and comfort. She'd cook dinner, give him a bath, they'd share a book, and then she'd rock her beautiful son to sleep.

Olivia went about starting dinner. As the oil in the pan began to sizzle, she heard the doorbell chime and Gage let out a squeal of delight. She shifted the pan to the back burner and hurried to the front room only to find Cade standing just beyond the locked screen door and Gage already standing there looking up at him, smiling.

A shot of anger burned through her before she'd noticed the smile on her son's face. The fact that Gage recognized him and, on his own, had run to the door to let him in wasn't a good thing in her mind. Cade Carter wasn't going to attach himself to some toddler, especially when that toddler belonged to her.

"What are you doing here?" The question was borderline rude—on second thought, it was spat out as rudely as she could have made it.

He lifted the new gallon of milk he carried in his hand and the other bag of groceries she'd left. "You left these in the fridge. I thought they might be dinner. I also took the liberty of getting a new gallon of milk for you. We used quite a bit at lunch."

Olivia let out a slow breath and an accompanied growl as she picked Gage up and rested him on her hip. "You didn't have to bring them over. I would have gotten more," she said as she unlocked the screen and pushed it open with her free hand.

Cade stepped in immediately and walked straight through the house to the kitchen as if leaving the groceries on the floor wasn't an option.

Olivia locked the door so Gage wouldn't accidently push it open and then followed Cade to the kitchen.

The moment she stepped through the door, Gage began reaching for Cade, who had set the bag on the table and even opened the refrigerator to set the milk inside. When he turned and saw Gage's arms open to him, he reached for him.

Olivia realized she was gripping Gage's legs tightly as Cade had to tug to release him from her grip.

"Hey, big guy," Cade said and Gage rested his head against his shoulder.

There was a pain that resonated in Olivia's chest. Of all the men in the world, Gage had to choose this one to be comfortable around? Well…why wouldn't he?

She moved past them both and back to the stove. She pulled the pan back over the burner and turned on the element again.

"I didn't mean to interrupt dinner." Cade moved in behind her, almost too close. "Chicken?"

"Yes."

"Homemade chicken. Can't tell you the last time I had that."

She could feel the words stinging the tip of her tongue. They were going to come out or choke her trying to keep them back. "Would you like to stay for dinner?"

"Yes." His answer was very quick, and when she turned to look at him, his smile was wide.

Why was he doing this to her? Couldn't he just be predictable and go home?

"Okay, get out of the kitchen and let me finish this then. I have a lot to do. I have to finish this and then I have to give Gage his bath and he has to get to bed."

"Let me give him his bath. It's the least I can do."

She was well aware that her jaw had dropped and her mouth hung open. She had to look like an idiot standing there sorting out his offer.

"You're going to give him a bath?"

"Sure. Can't be that hard, can it?"

Gage had sat up in his arms and was clapping his hands. "Dade. Bath."

She was sure they'd both stopped breathing. *Dade.* Her son's attempt at Cade...or dad?

She watched Cade's face as he registered the sentiment. His Adam's apple bobbed in his throat as he'd swallowed hard. "I'll get his bath." He turned and started down the hallway, obviously familiar with the house.

Olivia turned back to the stove, removed the pan from the heat again, and rested her hands against the counter. What was she doing?

A few minutes later she could hear the water running in the bathtub. Gage squealed at whatever it was that Cade had said to him. She didn't hear it as his voice was muffled from down the hall.

Olivia finished frying up the chicken, set it on a plate, covered it with a towel, and went to check on her son.

The bathtub was nearly full of bubbles. Gage's head and shoulders were all that were visible of him.

"Cade, how much soap did you put in there?"

He laughed. "Until he told me to stop."

She shook her head and looked down at the enormous man on the floor of the little bathroom. His shirt was soaking wet, and he was grinning from ear to ear watching her son blow handfuls of bubbles his direction.

"The bath was for one, Cade. Not two."

He looked down at himself. "Didn't even notice, really." He then shifted a glance up at her, his eyes taking their time to focus in on every inch of her body before they reached her face. "Did you come in here to join us?"

She cleared her mind and then her throat. Those eyes staring up at her meant no good and she knew it. "Dinner is almost ready."

"We still have to scrub." He took his eyes off of her and settled them back on Gage who blew another handful of bubbles his way. "Do you have a wash cloth?"

"Yes," she said, but it croaked out of her throat. "If you want to take that shirt off, I can dry it while we eat."

Cade gave her a nod and began to lift the white cotton T-shirt from his body. She wondered if the gasp was audible when she looked at him. Every muscle on his back was firm, his arms were sculpted, and his chest and abs chiseled.

He held out the shirt in his hand and smiled as he looked up at her. Yep, he'd heard her suck in that breath, and now she'd turn blue holding it.

Again, she cleared her throat. "I have to squeeze by you to get the wash cloth."

The bathroom was so small that she found herself having to balance against him, resting her hand on his bare skin. Her fingers gripped his shoulder as she reached past him to open the drawer with the wash cloth. Her thighs grazed his back, and she felt his body stiffen beneath her touch. Could he feel her tremble?

She grabbed the cloth and stood back up straight. When he looked up at her, his eyes were dark. Yes, he'd felt the tremble. When the corner of his mouth curved up, she worried that he'd read too much into it. Perhaps she'd read too much into it.

"I'll be in the kitchen. I'll finish up dinner." She hurried out the door before turning back. "His pajamas are in the top drawer of his dresser."

Cade watched Olivia hurry away. He'd never had a woman touch him so unassumingly, and the moment had been incredibly intimate.

He turned back to Gage who was quietly watching him as if he'd understood what had happened.

Gage smiled up at him and his chest tightened. He'd come back to Aspen Creek under protest. Never in his life would he have dreamed he'd be half naked in Olivia's bathroom, bathing her son, and waiting on dinner. It was a bit too domestic for his taste. So why did it feel so right?

He shook the thought from his head and went about finishing his job of getting Gage clean.

Once Gage was wrapped in a towel, Cade carried him down the hall until he found the bedroom with a crib and Disney characters on the wall. He set him in the crib and walked to the dresser. He pulled open the top drawer and pulled out the first pair of pajamas he found. As he shut the drawer, he noticed the picture frame on the top. His breath caught in his chest.

His shaking hands gripped the frame and he looked down at it. There were two pictures. In one, Olivia was in the hospital with Gage wrapped in a blanket and held close to her chest. She was happy and glowing.

It was the other picture that had his jaw clenching. There was his own father standing in the hospital holding a newborn Gage in his arms.

A stir of different emotions burst inside of him. Olivia was a mystery and entangled in his family. The smile on his father's face was nearly as wide as Olivia's, and the love in his eyes, holding the baby, hurt Cade. Had he looked at him like that? But it was then he noticed his father's bright eyes.

He turned and looked at Gage standing at the railing of the crib. His eyes.

He looked back down at the picture of his father. "Who is your daddy, little one?" he whispered to himself.

Olivia set the table as Cade walked into the kitchen with Gage in his pajamas. The sight of him holding her son was nearly as moving as the look of him.

She'd always thought he was handsome, but now he was also the sexiest man she'd ever seen and her body was acting strange when she looked at him, as if just that one touch would never be enough.

"You can set him in his chair." She pointed to the chair at the table with the plastic seat strapped to it.

Cade set Gage in the seat and strapped him in. He pushed him up to the table. "What can I help you with?"

The thought that Cade would offer to help with dinner amused her and a laugh escaped her. "What's funny."

"I just never thought I'd ask you to help me with dinner."

She turned to reach for the salad bowl and she felt him move in close behind her. His hand rested on her hip and his breath was on her neck.

"You know, I never thought you'd invite me to dinner either." He pressed closer against her and her breath hitched. His hand slid around to her stomach.

Cade reached out, picked up the bowl she'd had her hands on, and turned to set it on the table. She had to steady herself for a moment before turning to face her son and the man who was confusing every emotion she'd ever had.

As she turned, the sight of Cade at her table, seated next to Gage, gave her stomach a twist. It should have been the most familiar site. A man seated next to her child, prepared for dinner, giggling as they played with each other. But it was when they both looked up at her with those matching blue eyes that she thought she should just kick him out of the house. Any man could have walked into her life and she'd be satisfied. No, it had to be a Carter man.

Cade watched Olivia as she sat down at the table. Her lips were pursed, her shoulders straight, and her eyebrows were drawn together. He'd seen that face before. She was hiding something.

He wasn't sure what it was about seeing her again, but he didn't want to leave and just let her be. He didn't want to think that he'd be gone in a day and never see her again.

The overwhelming urge to hold her and ask her what was bothering her was taking over.

He reached for her hand and rested his atop hers. "Is everything okay?"

She sucked in a deep breath as though she was going to start yelling at him, but instead she looked up at Gage and let the breath out. "I'm fine."

Not another word was said, and she went about filling plates of food.

He'd managed to keep his seat between Gage and Olivia. She'd cut up Gage's food and Cade had helped him, but he knew she'd watched his every move, as if she were questioning his motives.

When dinner was finished, Olivia let Gage down from his chair and he began to pick up the plates.

"I can do that. It's late." She took the dishes from his hands.

"Olivia, what's wrong?"

"I can't have you here. It's confusing me."

She set the dishes in the sink and stood there.

Cade moved in closer. He wasn't going to let her hate him for the rest of his life. He wasn't sure why it was important, but it seemed to be.

He rested his hands on her shoulders and massaged them with his fingers. "Please, don't hate me. I didn't anticipate coming back here and wanting to spend more than a minute, but I'm enjoying your company."

"And tomorrow?"

"I'll still enjoy it."

She turned to face him and was nearly in his arms, but she slipped away and finished clearing the table. "You'll be planning your quick escape. We lost our friendship years ago, Cade. It wasn't important to you then, I can't imagine it would be important to you now."

"You have no idea…"

"I have a good idea." She opened the door to the refrigerator to return the milk and slammed it shut. "I can't have you here and look…" She stopped.

Gage was standing at his side, his arms wrapped around his leg. The moment lingered and the tension of her speech still hung in the air.

He picked up the toddler who rubbed his eyes and rested his head on his shoulder.

"I guess it's someone's bedtime."

Olivia reached out her arms to take him. "C'mon, baby. Mommy will take you to bed."

"No. Dade."

He could see the pulse in her temple and tears welling in her eyes. The right thing would have been to hand her son back to her and walk out of their lives, but his heart said differently.

"I'd like to say goodnight, if you don't mind me coming in with you."

Her eyes batted away the tears before she'd let them fall. She never was one to let someone see her cry.

"Fine. But then I think you'll need to go."

Chapter Six

Cade followed her closely to Gage's room and watched their routine. Gage played peek-a-boo with a small blanket over his head and would laugh when Olivia would find him under it. The joy was simple, and it warmed him like no other sight had.

After a few minutes of play, Gage yawned and rested his head against a stuffed animal he'd cuddled. Olivia rubbed the top of his head gently, and Gage's eyelids began to grow heavy. A few moments later, he was asleep and there was a peace in the room.

Olivia backed away from the crib slowly and headed for the door. Cade caught her arm and turned her toward the dresser. He pointed to the picture frame and watched as her eyes opened wide.

Immediately she pulled from him, left the room, and he followed. Once he was in the hallway with her, she pulled the door nearly closed and walked away toward the kitchen.

Suddenly dinner dishes seemed important, but she wasn't talking. He assumed that if they were married she'd go about doing what she was doing, in a huff, and ignoring him as if he weren't there at all. But that wasn't the case. He had some questions and he needed answers.

"You know, I'll help you with the dishes if you'll stop for a moment and talk to me."

"Cade, I don't want to talk to you. I don't know why I even invited you to have dinner with us."

She didn't look at him, but her words dripped with distain.

"I think, at this point, you could do me the courtesy of telling me why you lived with my father and why he was with you at the birth of your son."

Olivia dropped the pan she'd been scrubbing into the sink with a crash and her shoulders shook. He'd made her cry.

"None of this is your business. You need to get the estate settled and go home, Cade. There's nothing for you here."

If it were any other woman he'd have walked out the front door and let it slam behind him as he sped off in his fancy car. None of it mattered he told himself, but he knew that was a lie.

This was Olivia. The girl he'd shared the early years of his life with. The girl who helped him build that tree house that still stood in the back yard of his father's house. The same girl he'd shared all his childhood secrets with and, of course, the first girl he'd ever kissed.

Once all those thoughts ran through his head, he realized there was more. She was another misfit in the town without a parent. He had no mother, and she and Conner didn't know their fathers.

The three of them were a team. He was the leader. She was the brains. Conner was the follower without any say.

His chest ached, and he rubbed the palm of his hand down his breastbone to ease the pain.

Conner.

Conner was just another person Cade had jilted in his life and never looked back. The boy looked up to him. The young man needed him. The grown man was someone Cade had never known, and now he was gone.

The heat in the kitchen seemed to grow more intense. This wasn't how he wanted to walk away from her.

"Olivia, were you and my father…"

"Say it, Cade. The entire town has the same words dripping from their tongues. Why should you be any different?"

He stopped and watched her shoulders jerk with the sobs she tried to control.

Cade moved to her, turned her to him, and wrapped his arms around her. She seemed small against him—fragile. But at the same time he'd caused her so much pain, he felt the healing powers in holding the woman he'd fallen in love with as a child. Emotions quickly stirred in him that were unlike any he'd ever known before.

Her cheek nestled against his bare chest, and the dampness from her tears brushed against his skin.

When her breathing had calmed, she adjusted, letting him still hold her—comfort her. She raised her hands to his chest and let her palms warm against him.

His heart rate became faster, nearly uncomfortable. She shifted her head back and looked up at him. There was a need. A need to be accepted and cared for. He understood that need more than anyone could imagine. Wasn't that, after all, what had brought them together as friends?

Cade moved his hand from her back to her cheek. He brushed away the stray tears with his thumb. She sucked in a breath and he moved in.

There was not time to think before he pressed his lips to hers and pulled her in closer to him. Right in his arms was the woman he'd always known belonged there.

He'd expected some resistance, but he didn't get any. She opened her mouth to him, her lips were pliant, her tongue eager.

Olivia's arms moved around his neck and he eased them both against the counter, pressing their bodies closer together.

Once the fire of the kiss had been lit, he knew there'd be no stopping him—them.

Her fingers moved through his hair. Their kiss deepened, and he was sure it wasn't him who had done it.

She was as hungry as he was. At least that part he was familiar with.

He hoisted her up to his hips, wrapping her legs around him. She was like a doll in his arms. His doll. His responsibility.

The thought shook him, but her lips still worked against his. He carried her down the hallway, their mouths and tongues still entwined, and made his way to her bedroom.

As they walked through the door, he kicked it shut with his foot before moving Olivia up against it.

She arched against the door at her back, holding him tighter.

"Cade…" His name carried on her breath as he moved his lips to her neck. "What are we doing?"

"Oh, don't tell me you're going to stop me." He moved his lips to her ears. "But if you want me to, I'll stop."

She didn't speak right away.

Cade lifted his head away, still holding her against him. Her eyes settled on his.

"I don't think I want you to stop."

"That's what I wanted to hear." He moved his mouth against hers again, but the kiss was different now—hesitant. "You're thinking too hard."

"The last time I had sex with a man, I got Gage."

"Not a bad trade."

She sighed and rested her head against his shoulder. "No, it wasn't."

Of course, the thought crossed his mind that the last man she'd been with was his father. That was enough to ruin anyone's desire.

Instead of undressing her, the way he desperately wanted to, he carried her to the bed and sat her down.

"I've done enough to hurt you over the years. I'm not going to do that now."

"See," she chuckled, pushing a strand of hair from her eyes. "You should have gone when I told you too."

"I don't want to go now. I like looking at you in my shirt, though out of my shirt would be better."

She smiled. "I don't want you to go, but I don't think I can do this. The sex part."

He narrowed his eyes on her. "What else is there?"

"Stay the night. Let me sleep in your arms. At least when you're gone in a week I won't have lost anything, but maybe I'll have a good memory of time with a dear friend."

How could he deny her that logic?

It had been three o'clock when Olivia had awakened to check on Gage. He hadn't woken all night. It shouldn't have worried her, but it had.

The comforting part was, when she woke, she was still wrapped in Cade's arms.

Why she'd stopped him from making love to her, she didn't know. But, in her heart, she knew it was right. How could she give herself to another man who would make her leave, or who would leave her?

When she curled back up against him, he wrapped his arm around her.

"Everything okay?"

"Checking on Gage."

She felt him move against her. "He's okay, isn't he?" His voice had shot up, more alert.

There had never been a night in his short life in which he'd slept that long. "Never better."

"Hmmm," he nuzzled his lips to her neck and soon he was asleep again.

The next time she opened her eyes, the sun streamed through the curtains. She rolled to press her lips to Cade's, but he was gone.

Disappointment dropped into her stomach, and then the void was filled with anger. Why had she thought he'd be more than an average man? Thank goodness she hadn't given more of herself.

A moment later, she shot up from her pillow and ran out of the bedroom and down the hall. Gage. Gage wasn't awake. He hadn't had any terrors.

She burst through his door, and there he was sitting in his crib playing with a toy. He looked up at her and smiled before he stood and held out his arms to her.

"You had a good night, didn't you?" She picked him up and held him close to her.

Gage would never leave her or break her heart. At least she had that.

Only a moment later, the doorbell rang. She looked at the small digital clock on the dresser next to the picture of Gage and Austin. It was seven-thirty.

A surge of hope raced through her. Perhaps he'd only gone out—a run maybe, no—coffee. Yes, that must have been it.

Olivia hurried to the front door with Gage wrapped in her arms. She flung open the front door and standing there, on the other side of the screen, was her mother.

She let out what she knew was an ungrateful sigh. "Mom, I didn't expect you."

"I just got back into town. Of course, you are my first stop."

Of course she was. Olivia pushed open the screen and looked past her to the driveway. His car was gone. Well, at least her mother hadn't seen him coming out of her bedroom.

Her mother reached out her hands. "Look at my grandson. Come see Grandma."

Gage turned his face into his Olivia's shoulder.

"Oh, he doesn't know me. See, you keep me from him."

"I do not. You're never around. I haven't seen you in almost two months." She turned and headed toward the kitchen, her mother close behind. "Where have you been?"

"Oh, you know. Here. There. It's a good thing I ran into Cade at the store. He said you weren't living with Austin anymore, but had bought this place."

Olivia set Gage in his high chair and turned to make coffee. She hoped her mother didn't see the shock that had forced her eyes open wide. "You saw Cade at the store?"

She could hear her mother rifling around in her purse. "He said he was on donut detail this morning. But then he left the store without anything. I didn't know he was back in town. Is that why you're not with Austin anymore? Cade moved in and disrupted your cozy living arrangement?" There was a snide tone to her voice. Her mother made her point perfectly clear.

"Austin died mom and I lived there, I wasn't *with* him." She turned and saw the cigarette between her mother's lips. "Mom, don't light that. Gage…"

"Oh, relax." Her mother put the cigarette back in her purse. "So, Austin died, huh?"

"I'm sure you knew that."

"Yeah, I'm sure I heard something about it." She examined her perfect, red manicure. "How come he didn't let you stay in the house? Seems like you two were so close." She gave a wave of her hand in the air. "You always were, that is. I never thought it was an appropriate relationship."

Olivia turned back to the coffee maker and set her jaw. Even her own mother didn't respect her. Not that it shocked her any. Olivia was never Celeste Baker's top priority. That was how she grew so close to Austin and

Cade, after all. How many nights had Celeste gone out all night and left her home alone?

She took two mugs out of the cupboard and set them on the counter.

Olivia had figured out years ago, when she was still a young girl, that Celeste's problem with Austin wasn't his relationship with her daughter. It was that when she'd made her own play, or plays as it was, he'd never noticed. He was much too busy raising his son, his nephew, and taking care of her daughter to think about rolling in the sheets with Celeste. All it had done was prove to be a challenge and a source of aggravation until Celeste married again.

Just the thought of that sent a chill down Olivia's spine. Thank goodness for Carter men when it came to Celeste's ex-husband. Without them, Olivia wouldn't be standing in her own kitchen, cringing at her mother.

"This is a nice place, sweetheart. How do you afford it?"

Olivia picked up the coffee pot and slowly poured coffee into each mug. "I have a good job, Mother."

"Right. Parker Woods always did like you."

"I have a degree in finance. It has nothing to do with Parker's feelings for me."

"Hmmm." Her mother purred out as Olivia pulled a sippy cup from the cupboard and then opened the refrigerator and pulled out the milk. Her mother looked up at her. "Oh, Cade said he'd have to stop by and see you to say hi. I'm surprised you didn't see him at the funeral. I heard you arranged everything."

Olivia bit back the smile. Her mother didn't even realize she'd passed on a message.

He hadn't run out on her in the middle of the night. He'd gone for breakfast, but had run into her mother. Even Cade knew that wasn't a good sign.

Perhaps he had changed. She let the smile surface on her lips, but only momentarily. It had been a very long time since Olivia looked forward to seeing Cade again, and this time perhaps she wouldn't let him only sleep.

Clearing her mind, Olivia poured the milk into the cup, tightened on the lid, and set it in front of Gage. He scooped it up and went about drinking it.

"I did arrange Austin's funeral. There was no one around to do it."

"What about that sister of his? Last I saw her she was in Vegas." Which meant Celeste had been, too.

"You know, she's gone." Olivia thought better of it. "Or was. I think she was here long enough to empty the house of a few things while we were all at the funeral."

Her mother gave her a slow nod. "So Cade just let you do all the work?"

She wasn't going to sell Cade out, not at this point. "It was my pleasure to do it, Mom."

"I'll bet it was." The words were said under her breath, but not completely hidden.

The vile taste of distain filled Olivia's mouth. "So, how come you showed back up now?"

"A woman wants to see her grandson from time to time." She brushed her hand over Gage's head. "Why don't you let me take him for the morning? I'll go get him a donut or something sweet. That's what Grandmas do, right?"

"Mom, he doesn't need anything like that."

"Well, it would give you a moment to get out of that nasty T-shirt and get a shower."

Olivia let out a long breath. She wasn't going to get into it with her own mother. But there was more, and it didn't take rocket science to quickly figure out that her mother thought Olivia was going to get something out of Austin's estate.

She lifted her coffee mug to her lips and looked at Gage. Olivia had everything she ever needed in life, and thanks to Austin, it was all securely hers. She didn't need anything else. It was all Cade's.

The coffee scorched her throat when she swallowed hard. Yep, it was all Cade's, and he'd soon be throwing it all into boxes or dumpsters and heading back to his life in Wisconsin.

Chapter Seven

Olivia's mood had quickly soured after her mother's visit. The offer had been made, because that's what good daughters do, for her to stay with them during her visit. But even Celeste knew it would be better to get a room in town. After all, Olivia was a bit too old fashioned when it came to her own mother bringing strangers home from the bar. Not that those words had been said aloud, but they both knew the implications.

Olivia shook her head as she washed down the kitchen table. That wasn't fair. Perhaps her mother had changed. Then again, maybe she hadn't.

She scrubbed harder as she thought that she missed Austin much more than she'd ever missed her mother. Celeste Baker never seemed to be quite far enough away, except when Olivia had moved back to Grand Junction before Gage was born. She had been quite surprised to find she was a grandmother, and Olivia had been just as surprised to find her mother had been in jail that whole time.

Her negative thoughts shifted when the phone rang. She reached for the receiver and answered it.

"I saw your mom's car drive over the bridge. I figured it was safe to call."

She had been so angry all morning, Olivia couldn't have imagined that Cade's voice on the other end of the phone would actually put her at ease.

She slid into one of the chairs at the table and relaxed. "I got your message."

"Good. I didn't want you to think I snuck away."

She didn't confirm that that had been a thought.

"I thought you'd like breakfast in bed," he continued. "I figured when I ran into your mom at the store that she'd be headed your way. I thought she'd left town years ago."

It surprised her that he knew that, but then again, when she'd left it was under the black cloud of scandal. Not that that was a new story in the life of Celeste Baker.

"She seems to have just shown up for the first time in months."

"Hey, listen, I was thinking I owe you a couple meals." Thank goodness he changed the subject. "Why don't I burn some steaks on the grill for dinner? You and Gage come over and spend the night here."

Olivia bit down on her bottom lip. That sure was a mixed invitation. "We would love to come for dinner, though burning steaks doesn't sound like a cooking method."

He laughed. "You haven't seen me bar-b-que."

"But, about the other part…"

"Olivia, I want to spend more time with you. With both of you. I've missed you, and I didn't realize just how much."

She couldn't decide if that was reason to pursue the invitation—to find out what he meant—or reason enough to reject it. After all, after the age of twelve, Cade Carter had been nothing to her but a thorn in her side—and an unsatisfied ache in her heart.

"I can't set Gage up like this." The maternal instincts were ramped up now. "He can't get used to you. You're going to leave."

"I'm in no hurry. In case you didn't hear, I'm a washed up, injured football player. No one wants one of those."

"Cade…"

"It's okay. You nearly die on the field holding tight to that damn ball, and moments later, your career is over.

They write you a check, tell you maybe they'll consider you for a coaching position, and the next minute they're having a press conference telling the world they just signed some new hot shot. It's how the game is played."

Though he was joking, she wondered how much pain there really was behind the words.

"What time would you like us there?"

"How about five?"

"We'll see you then."

"Olivia, plan to stay."

The line went dead, but her heart kicked into gear. What was she getting herself into?

Cade watched Olivia and Gage unload from the car. It was a sight that had caught him off guard. A mother and her son. The glances. The touches. The smiles they exchanged. He didn't remember his mother. He'd missed out on a lot, he saw that now.

He limped down the front steps to the car, and Gage reached for him. He took him from Olivia's arms and held him against his chest.

"That looks like a diaper bag." He nodded to the bag she pulled from the floor of the car. "When I said plan to stay, I meant pack a bag."

"Cade, I can't start up some affair with you just because you're here. All of this is awkward. I think dinner is a good place to leave it."

"I'm not trying to hurt you," he found himself whispering as though someone else would hear. "C'mon, what happened between us that we can't enjoy each other as adults?"

"Life happened. You haven't really talked to me since the day you kissed me in the tree house."

He smiled and touched her face. "My first kiss. Not one I've ever forgotten."

She pursed her lips. "Cade, that was a different life. This one is more serious. I have him to think about. You have your life back in Green Bay. I'm not asking you to come home and take over your dad's place."

He knew she meant that figuratively and realistically. "It's a good house. I could rent it out, or keep it to come back to."

"When? When you needed someone? Not when they needed you?"

Whatever had happened to this woman after that kiss in the tree house, she had no intentions of trusting him or letting him into her life.

"You're not even going to try to trust me, are you?"

"I haven't had a lot of practice in trusting men. Or you."

"Some of us change."

"And some don't." She dropped the diaper bag back in the car. "This is a mistake, Cade." She reached her arms out for Gage. "We should just go. You should finish fixing up the house, sell it, close out his accounts, and get back to your life. Gage and I need to…"

He couldn't take anymore of her common sense. He moved in and planted a firm kiss on her lips.

She pulled back. "Not in front of him." She glanced at Gage.

"He needs to know someone else thinks the world of you, too." He looked at Gage. "I have something for you."

He headed toward the garage with Gage still in his arms, and he could hear Olivia grunt as she reached back into the car for the diaper bag, slammed the car door shut, and followed them.

Cade opened the side door to the garage and set Gage on the floor in front of an old, antique pedal car. Immediately Gage hurried over to the toy and climbed in.

"Cade, that is wonderful. Where did you find it?"

"Dad had it buried in the back of the garage under a tarp with all of Conner's things."

The smile on her face diminished. "It was Conner's?"

"Yeah, I'd forgotten all about it. I think he had it when he was Gage's age. Seems like it broke when we were about five. His mom beat his ass for it." The words had come out before the feelings hit him. The car broke because of him, not Conner. Conner had paid for that, and Cade had never told a soul.

He cleared his throat. "I fixed it up. It's his now."

"Oh, no." She was quick to reject his gift. "He can't have it. It's not his."

"I want him to have it. Dad would want him to have it."

Olivia walked out of the garage. Again, he had her in tears. Most women would slap him across the face and leave him to move on to the next woman in line. This one was different.

"C'mon, big guy, let's drive this on the driveway."

He helped Gage out of the car and pushed it out in front of the garage. Olivia was on the back porch wiping her eyes.

Gage quickly figured out the pedals and was off, giggling and driving about. Cade slowly walked up the few steps to the back porch, watched Gage climb from the car and try to turn it around before getting back in, and then walked toward the grill and turned it on.

"Dad must have cooked out here not too long ago. The grill plate was clean, and the propane bottle was full."

Olivia looked out over the driveway. "We celebrated his birthday. Sixty was certainly too young for him to die."

"He'd turned sixty?" He closed the lid to the grill. "I don't think I ever knew how old my dad was." He sat down in the chair next to her, but she kept an eye on Gage. "I don't think I knew much about him at all."

"It's not too late."

He sat back in the chair and rubbed his knee. It ached as bad as his heart did. "I suppose I'll know plenty when I start going through all the things here."

"He had a full life before he settled here."

"You've talked to him a lot about that, huh?"

"He's all I had, Cade. I know that probably makes you mad, but…"

"No. Not mad. Sad that I wasn't a good son. I always blamed him for that."

Now she turned around and her eyes narrowed on him. "You blame him for your lack of compassion?"

She deserved to be angry. He was angry at himself, too. "I always did. I had it in my head that he drove my mother away. If a mother didn't even want her son, the father must have been horrible."

Olivia shook her head. "He loved her. She just couldn't love him back."

"So why have his son?"

He watched her take in a deep breath and then look out over the driveway at Gage. "He said she thought she could change." She turned back to him. "She thought she could try to do the domestic life, small town, man at home and a baby. She was wrong."

"Nice. You know more about my mother than I do."

"I asked."

Cade knew that was more than he'd ever done. He'd never asked where his mother was. He'd only accused his father of pushing her away. However, his father never argued that either.

"What about Gage's dad? Did you love him?"

She looked down at her hands which were folded in her lap. "I thought so. He'd always been there when I needed someone."

The subject caused her an enormous amount of pain and wasn't very comfortable for him either. If he pursued the conversation, he just might find out that little boy he'd fallen in love with was his brother. He wasn't ready for that. He wanted Olivia to himself.

"Conner was in the Army?" he asked, breaking the awkward silence that had developed.

"Marines."

Cade nodded. "I found his duffle bag in the garage with the rest of his things." He looked across the back yard at the burned out foundation of the house Conner had lived in. He took a breath and asked, "When did Conner die?"

Olivia lifted her head and looked at the house, too. "A few months after your accident."

"He came to see me, didn't he?"

She nodded. "You said you didn't know him. You had security escort him from the hospital."

At the very mention of the accident, his neck hurt, his head throbbed, and even more his heart ached. "I was on so many pain medications I didn't know who I was. But, somewhere, I've always known he was there. I wish I could tell him I was sorry."

Olivia only nodded her head and then turned her attention back to Gage. "Your dad was there, too."

He reached his hand to her arm, and she turned back to him. "My dad? No one ever told me he was there."

"He asked them not to. Someone named Ashley got him into your room so he could spend some time with you while you were sedated. He asked them not to tell you. He figured it would just upset you and set you back."

Cade ran his hand over his head and let it sink in. Were there two more stubborn men in the world than him and his father?

He stood from his seat and headed into the house, without another word, to start dinner and get a grip on his emotions.

Olivia cried when he walked inside. There was so much Cade needed to know about his father. The man loved him. He just was a man and couldn't show it. The only time he'd ever loved someone they'd left him so, of course, he was going to be afraid to show love, even to his son. But the truth was he was proud of Cade, and Cade needed to know that.

She watched Gage climb from the car and push it around. He was safe and content in Austin's driveway for a moment. She stood and walked into the house.

Cade was at the sink mixing a salad. Steaks sat on a plate next to him, seasoned and ready for the grill.

She walked up behind him and wrapped her arms around him. "I didn't mean to upset you."

He clasped his hands over hers. "This whole journey has been upsetting. I miss him, and I realize I didn't even know him."

He turned and gathered her in his arms. "Tell me, were you in love with him?"

"Cade…" She tried to pull away, but he held her close.

"No. I need to know."

Olivia pushed away and paced the kitchen while he watched. "Once, maybe. One of those foolish girl things." She shook her head. "He wasn't one for scandal." She wanted to laugh, but, in her heart, she couldn't. She took a breath to explain her silly, childhood crush when they heard Gage scream, and they both ran out the back door and to the driveway.

Gage stood near the end of the driveway behind the truck, which had done some off roading and gotten stuck in the rocks. He pulled and he pushed and he screamed again.

Once Olivia's heart stopped pounding, and she could catch her breath, she could laugh.

Cade walked over to the car and pulled it from the rocks. "It really isn't four wheel drive, buddy."

Gage gave him a knowing nod and climbed back in and pedaled off.

Cade looked up at her. It was going to break her heart into a million pieces when he went back to his life. But standing there in the driveway, his eyes matching those of her son and his heart exposed by the smile on his face, she couldn't help but love him—this time as a woman.

She walked across the driveway, wrapped her arms around his neck, and pulled him in for a deep and satisfying kiss.

"You're going to break my heart, aren't you?"

"Never on purpose," he said in her ear as he held her tight.

"We will stay with you." She inched back to look at him. "And I know my heart is going to shatter, but don't hurt Gage. He's already trusting you. You can't hurt him."

Cade looked up to where Gage rode around in a circle. "I didn't know a grown man could fall in love with someone other than a woman." He looked back down at her. "I'd never hurt him. I promise."

Well, he'd given her his word. She just wondered how good his word actually was.

Chapter Eight

Olivia sat down at her desk on Monday morning and sifted through the papers she'd left there on Saturday afternoon.

Again, her mind wasn't on her work. It was on Cade.

This time, however, she was smiling.

He'd given her son a priceless gift and, even though it had pained him physically, he'd even carried him up to the tree house. He'd cooked her an amazing dinner. And then, while her son slept in his own crib in the first home he'd known, Cade had made love to her all night, gently and sweetly, in his old bedroom which his father had kept pristine.

Her entire body still tingled at the thought of every touch, every kiss, and every flowing movement between them. He'd taken her to the edge and then fallen over with her. Then he'd held her, caressed her skin, and whispered sweet things in her ear. Things only Cade Carter would know she'd want to hear. She wasn't a fool to think it would last forever, but she was going to enjoy every moment she had.

Parker tapped on her door. "Good morning."

"Good morning." She smiled up at him.

"You look refreshed."

"I am. New week. Time for moving on."

He nodded and then shut her office door behind him. "Listen, I know this isn't any of my business, but I heard Kat talking and…" He rubbed the back of his neck. "I know Cade has been staying at your place, and last night you stayed at his."

Olivia gritted her teeth. "I didn't realize who slept in my bed had anything to do with my job." Her voice had risen to a pitch she'd never wanted to use around her boss.

"Oh, no." He looked up at her, his eyes wide. "No, nothing like that. I just wanted to say that if you're involved with Cade then I'm sorry about the invitation to have pizza the other day. I didn't mean to step over any boundaries."

Olivia dropped her shoulders. "Parker, Cade is an old friend."

"Oh, I know. You two were very close once. I just didn't know you still were."

He was right. There was no reason for anyone to think that she and Cade had anything left in common except for his father. "Thanks for the invite anyway."

He nodded. "Sure. If you need anything, let me know."

The door to her office opened again and Kat stuck her head in. "Hey, darling, your boyfriend is here."

"Mrs. McCormick, he's a customer of this bank. Not my boyfriend." How was it the woman could be so endearing and so crass at the same time.

"Right. I'll send him in."

Cade walked through the door a moment later, nearly running Parker over.

"Good morning, Cade."

"Parker." He slipped his sunglasses behind his head as Parker shot her a glance and shut the door.

She tried to push past his obviously foul mood. "Good morning, sir." She smiled and pushed up from her chair to reach across the desk to kiss him, but when he looked up at her and narrowed his eyes, she relaxed into her seat. "What can I do for you?"

"I need a checking account."

"We can do that." She opened the drawer with the necessary papers in it. "Why do you need this?"

"It seems as though no one in this town takes credit, and an out-of-state check is out of the question."

"What are you writing checks for?"

"I have to get that house fixed up. Already this morning, I've had three contractors there to give me bids. One won't take my check, and the other two came in much higher than the other. Both have made comments that they knew me, and I dated their daughters. Neither of which I remember, but hell, I guess this town has its opinion of me."

He had certainly soured her mood.

"Do you really think the people in this town are just trying to mess with you? I mean really you…"

"Didn't even show up for my own father's funeral."

How could she argue with that logic?

She collected the information she needed, and Cade filled out and signed the necessary papers.

"Well, Mr. Carter, you are officially a new customer of this bank."

"Great." He took the papers she'd tucked into the bank envelope for him and shoved them into his back pocket. "I have some business to take care of. I'll be gone a few days. Keep an eye on the house?"

Her mouth opened and she shut it quickly. So much for the nice, warm good morning he'd given her. Officially he'd frozen her out. "Sure."

"Great. Thanks."

And, with that, he put on his sunglasses and headed out of the bank.

Olivia balled her fists to her side. She walked directly down to Parker's office. "Is that dinner invitation still open?"

He looked up at her and nodded. "Of course."

"I think we should do it soon. Tonight?"

"Yeah. Sure."

"Great. I'll meet you there at six."

He nodded again. "What about Cade?"

Olivia held up her hand. "Do you see a wedding ring on this finger?" With that she walked away. Oh, she'd been so stupid.

Cade had started out of town much later than he'd wanted. At this rate, he wouldn't hit Las Vegas until the wee hours of morning. He was sure his aunt would be awake, but perhaps not home. He'd have to get a motel room and rest up. This certainly wasn't what he'd wanted to deal with.

He'd hoped Olivia would show up after work. He'd had half a mind to invite her along, but his aunt was nasty and Olivia didn't need that. Besides, he'd been in such a bad mood when he'd gone to the bank that he wouldn't blame her if she didn't talk to him at all.

Cade rolled over the Rose Bridge and headed out of town, but a quick glance at his gas tank and he knew he wouldn't be getting far. He checked his watch again. It was seven-thirty. Maybe he should just wait until tomorrow to leave.

He pulled into the 7-11 and stopped the car in front of the pumps. It hurt to get out of the damn car. As soon as he was back in Green Bay he was selling the stupid thing to Ashley. That had always been the deal anyway.

He opened the door to the tank, started the pump, and waited. It was then Olivia's car caught his eye. A moment later, she walked out of the pizzeria across the street with Gage on her hip, and he was screaming.

It broke his heart to think Gage wasn't happy. But to see him warmed him to the core.

A moment later, Parker Woods exited the restaurant with two children, one on each side. Cade had no idea how old children were supposed to look, but they didn't look very old at all. Each of them had one of his hands and tugged in two different directions.

He watched as Olivia buckled Gage in the car, and Parker unlocked his car and the two children at his side hurried in.

But then he watched Parker and Olivia each walk to the back of their cars which were parked next to each other. The conversation was intimate, not the kind where they were talking about a bank loan—that much he could tell. The air in his lungs nearly stuck there when he watched Parker reach for Olivia's hand and then he moved in and kissed her on the cheek.

What in the hell was going on? One night with him and the next night with Parker? What kind of game was Olivia playing?

All of this only days after his father died, and hadn't she admitted to having feelings for his father?

Well, he'd been dumb enough to fall for her charm and drag her to bed. Shit! He cared for that little boy, and he was just a ploy in her game.

The gas pump shut off, and Cade quickly hung up the hose, closed the tank door, and climbed back into the car. With a thunderous noise, he peeled out of the parking lot of 7-11 and headed out of town. From his review mirror, he could see her head snap up. He'd made his point.

Chapter Nine

It had been the worst night ever. Gage was awake nearly all night screaming. She'd hoped the two nights without the night terrors was the signal of the end.

She combed her hair and looked over her reflection in the mirror. Dark circles plagued her eyes.

Simply put, it was going to be a very long day.

Michelle had suggested Gage spend the day with his grandmother, and though Olivia didn't like the idea, she agreed.

Her mother met her at the door to her hotel room, all dolled up for the day.

"You remember Mary Ann? Her granddaughter is visiting today so we're going to meet at the park."

"Please be careful with him. He's all I have."

"You're still alive, aren't you?" Her mother reached for Gage. "I know what I'm doing."

Gage tried to pull back from his grandmother, but when she had him in her arms, Olivia took a step back.

"I'll be done right at five."

"I'll be here. But don't be late. I have an interview for a job."

"You're getting a job?"

"Sure. I'm sticking around. The bar needs a new bartender. Sounds like my kind of job."

It sure did, and Olivia realized she didn't want her mother there. Aspen Creek was her home. There was no room for Celeste Baker there.

Gage reached out for her again, and she had to just turn and leave. That moment had broken Olivia's heart nearly as much as driving by Austin's house and seeing Cade's car still gone.

Parker was waiting for her the moment she walked into the bank. He followed her into the office and closed the door behind him.

"Is something wrong, Parker?"

"Listen, I didn't mean any harm last night when I kissed you. I mean, wow, I didn't…"

"Stop. It's nothing. It wasn't like we made out. It was a peck on the cheek."

"So Cade is okay?"

She shrugged. "He left town."

"Oh, God, I'm so sorry."

She watched Parker pace back and forth. "Parker, let it go. After all, the whole night didn't quite turn out like we'd thought."

He looked at her and chuckled. "I'm not sure they'll ever let us back in that restaurant."

She laughed. "I've never seen three little kids make such a mess. Gage usually isn't that much work."

"If it's any consolation, my daughter loved you. She might have spilled her entire soda on you, but she thought you were really nice."

"Thanks. Maybe someday we can have dinner at my house. Then the kids can run around and no one will be bothered."

"I think my kids would enjoy that." He walked closer to her and took her hand in his. "What about us? Do you think…"

He was so close she placed her hand on his chest. "Parker, listen, I don't think we should…"

"I know. Cade, right?" He took a step back. "If you need someone, I'm here."

He opened the door and left her alone to think about the confused state she was in. How had it all come to this?

Cade watched the ceiling fan spin above him. He must have found the cheapest, dirtiest motel outside of Vegas. Not that it had mattered. He hadn't slept all night. The image of Gage so upset, followed by Parker kissing Olivia, had his stomach tied in knots.

Perhaps he'd overstepped the boundaries by making moves on Olivia. But he hadn't been the only one in that bed the other night. No, she'd matched him move for move as they made love all night long. He'd never felt so connected with a woman—ever.

Then again, no other woman had been Olivia. In his heart, he'd waited his whole life to hold her.

He looked at the clock on the nightstand. After a shower and a cheap Vegas breakfast, he'd head to his aunt's house. Hopefully she'd have the papers he needed to close out his father's estate. Then he could decide how to handle Olivia. But first he'd better call Ashley. It was going to be a few more days before he'd be home.

Cade pulled into the trailer park complex that matched his aunt's address. He knew the specific trailer the moment he pulled up in front of it.

He stepped out of his car and saw the curtains in the window move. She'd seen him already. There was no turning back.

Only a few moments later, his aunt opened the front door and stood there in a ratty bathrobe with slippers on her feet and a cigarette in her fingers.

"I figured I'd see you sooner or later." Her voice crackled as she spoke.

"It seems I need a few things from you."

She nodded as she considered him. "Fancy car."

"Thank you."

"Money must be nice." She walked back into the house, and Cade limped up the stairs to follow.

The house was packed with miscellaneous items in uneven piles. There wasn't an uncluttered surface. The air was thick, and the stench of stale smoke and cat hair clogged his lungs.

"The postmaster said you might have the mail from Dad's house."

She took a long drag from her cigarette and nodded. "Have a seat."

She pointed to a cleared spot on the couch and then disappeared into the kitchen.

Cade hesitantly sat down. He could hear his aunt shuffling around in the other room, moving papers.

He noticed the TV on the makeshift table in the corner. No doubt it was the TV she took from his father's house.

When she came back into the room she had an envelope in her hand. "I assume this is what you're looking for."

He took it and looked inside. "Yes. Thank you."

"I don't suppose he had much left for you. The house is falling apart, and he'd given all his money to that girl that used to live next door to him."

"Olivia?"

She nodded as she took another drag from her cigarette. "She had her claws in him." She looked him in the eye. "Already been in a fight? Or did she give you the black eye for showing up?"

Cade touched the skin around his eye. He'd nearly forgotten about the bruise—or the fight which had ensued over something said about Conner.

His aunt examined the burning ash at the tip of her cigarette. "You know, that relationship your father had with her wasn't natural. She was just using him. Just as she used everyone around her. Must have learned it from her mother. You're not the first visitor I've had this week, you know."

Cade shoved the papers into his back pocket. He tried to breathe through his frustration. "You don't know what you're talking about."

"Hmm," she tightened her lips. "She was always around. Even when she was younger. Then he hid her away in Grand Junction when things got too serious between her and my son."

She took a drag from the cigarette burning in her hands and then took another out of the pocket of her robe and lit it with the stub of the other cigarette.

"Conner? She was involved with Conner?" His jaw was hurting from clenching it. "She didn't mention that."

"She drove him to drink and eventually kill himself in that house your dad thought he was saving us in. What a dump that was."

He couldn't imagine that he was even related to this woman. "You said Dad gave all his money to her. How do you know this?"

She let out a grunt and pulled out another envelope from her pocket. "His latest will. Seems he bought her the house she lives in now."

Cade looked at the front of the envelope. It had Olivia's name written on it in his father's handwriting, and it had been opened. Inside was his father's will and the numbers to his bank accounts at the bank in Aspen Creek.

He didn't have time to stand there in the filth of his Aunt's house and read the entire will, but it was clear enough. Everything his father owned now belonged to Olivia and Gage. Everything but his house and the contents of the safety deposit box at the bank.

Cade swallowed hard. He noticed there was another form in the envelope, and he pulled it out. When he looked up at his aunt, there was a crooked grin on her lips.

"You met her little boy?"

He knew she meant Gage and he nodded.

"Seems to have Carter eyes. He looks just like my daddy."

Cade looked down at the piece of paper shaking between his fingers. It was a copy of Gage Baker's birth certificate—and his Cade's father's name was on it.

Chapter Ten

It had been three days since Olivia had awakened in Cade's arms. She missed him.

She drove by the house four times a day. There had been a few workers there painting the exterior of the house, but no sign of Cade or his car.

Gage continued to be awake all night having nightmares, but now he'd begun to yell for Dade.

Cade had promised not to break her baby's heart, but he was doing just that. Not to mention, she was a wreck, too.

Her back was turned to her office door as she worked on the computer. She heard it open and close. "Parker, I'm very busy."

"Yeah, and I'll bet meeting you behind closed doors is just what he was waiting for."

She spun around in her chair when she heard Cade's voice, but there was nothing she could think of to say.

"I got the papers. Let's close this damn thing." He threw the envelope on the desk and fell into the chair below him.

Olivia reached for the envelope. "This has my name on it."

"Sure does." The pulse in his neck quickened. "Seems like I was written out of his will. All except the house and the safety deposit box."

Olivia took the papers out of the envelope and looked them over. "Cade, this doesn't make any sense. I protest. I don't want anything."

"He bought you a damn house." He slapped his hand down on her desk. "You were already getting everything out of him." He was up and out of the chair, pacing her office.

She stood to meet him. "I didn't ask him to. He asked me to leave his house, and he said he'd lend me the money to buy my own house."

"Lend?"

"Please listen to me." She pressed her fingers to her lips. "I had already decided that I'd pay you back. That money should have been yours. He'd saved it for you."

"And yet, somehow, you managed to get it from him? Is this how you work? Did your mother teach you how to manipulate men like this?"

Any counter attack stuck in her throat. She tried to breathe around it but only found it was making her dizzy, so she sat down in the chair Cade had occupied earlier. "I didn't want this. You have to understand, I didn't ask him to do this. I don't want it."

Cade turned his back to her and watched the traffic out on the road in front of the bank. "You didn't tell me about you and Conner."

She gasped, and he turned to look at her.

"So that is true, huh? You've had your share of all of us?"

"Oh, Cade." She stood. "You don't know what you're talking about. I didn't do anything wrong."

"He killed himself? I thought he died in a fire."

The tears were rolling down her cheeks now. There was nothing she could do to control them. "He did."

"My aunt seems to think you had something to do with that."

She could only shake her head. What could she really tell him about Conner at this moment? "I will close out the account, and the money is yours."

"Great."

"Do you have the key to the safety deposit box?"

Cade grunted out a laugh. "All business, huh? No, I don't have the key."

"I'm sure I can get Parker to…"

He stepped right up to her. "I'm sure you can get Parker to do anything."

She sucked in a breath, but their conversation was stopped by a knock at the door. Parker opened it slightly.

"Is everything okay in here?"

"Everything is fine," she quickly spat out.

"It's more than fine. It's done." Cade slipped back on his sunglasses and walked out of her office and out of the bank.

"Did he hurt you?" Parker moved in, closing the door behind him. "I'll kill him if he hurt you."

"No. No, just my ego." She looked into Parker's worried eyes. "I seem to fall in love with the wrong guys, don't I?"

Parker let out a breath and took a step back. "You're in love with him? Even after all of that?" She narrowed her eyes at him and he shrugged. "The walls in this place are paper thin. I didn't mean to overhear."

Olivia nodded. "Parker, my problem is I've been in love with the jerk since I was six."

"What about you and Austin?"

Of course he'd ask.

Olivia shook her head. "He was a father to me. Anyone who thinks differently is just small-minded."

"I'm sorry for having considered it then."

"I can't blame you." She walked back around to the other side of her desk and turned off the screen on her computer. "Listen, I know this comes at a very bad time, with the festivities of the fourth coming up and all, but I need a few days off."

"I don't know…"

"Parker, I need to sort this part of my life out."

He gave her a nod, and she quickly gathered her belongings, the envelope from her desk, and then headed out the door.

Cade's car was parked out front of the house and the painters' vans were still in the driveway. She hurried up the front steps, skirting around ladders and paint cans.

The house smelled of paint fumes even though all the windows were open. There were boxes stacked in the living room, labeled to be given away.

When Cade finally walked down the stairs with another box, she was standing there. "You've been busy this morning."

"I've been here all week." His words were sharp and pierced her, just as she assumed he'd meant to.

She moved toward him, anger swarming in her belly. "You've been here all week and you didn't tell me? You promised not to hurt us, Cade. This is exactly why I knew going to bed with you was the wrong thing to do."

"You have some room to talk. You brought this on yourself, you know."

"I've done nothing."

He let out a grunt and dropped the box in his hands. She heard the crash of the items inside. "What is that?"

"Trophies, they don't mean squat. None of it does."

She tried to move her focus away from the fact he was able to throw away the life his father had kept preserved. But Cade obviously never had thought that was too important.

"Your father thought it was important."

"I don't need to hear how he was proud of me and loved me. I know I was a sorry excuse for a son." He ran his hands over his head. "I can't believe he'd keep any of this stuff." He looked at the boxes on the floor that surrounded them.

"What is all this?"

"Everything from my room and some of the boxes from the basement."

Olivia swallowed hard. "You disassembled your room?"

"Can't sell a house with a trophy room intact, can you?"

That made it very official. He wasn't staying—never had intended to.

"Cade, about what happened the other night..."

"You don't owe me an explanation. Parker has always had you in his sights, and I did nothing but hurt you for years."

"That's not true."

He bit his lip. "I remember so clearly the day you moved away from that house next door. I'd heard you cry all night from your bedroom. You hid in our tree house, and I climbed up and promised I'd run away with you."

Olivia bit back the tears that threatened to form. "I remember."

"You let me hold you. You'd never let me get that close to you before." Cade picked up a box from the floor and set it on top of the one he'd dropped earlier. "I kissed you."

"Yes, you did."

He turned to her. His eyes were sad and she couldn't tell what he was thinking.

He raised his hand to her cheek and held it there. "My first kiss and it was with the girl I loved."

Olivia's mouth opened, but there were no words. She had to process what he'd said. "Cade, after that day you told me you hated me."

"I know." He dropped his hand. "I did hate you. I hated that you left me here alone."

"It wasn't my choice."

"No, your mother's husband. But I didn't see it that way. You, Dad, and Conner were my stability. When you left Conner didn't come around as much. Dad had to work as usual, and you weren't right there."

"You were quick enough to replace me as your friend."

"Junior high is supposed to be a bitch." He laughed, but she didn't.

"It was the only time I had in town. Aside from that, I was locked up in that nasty trailer with that horrible man."

Her voice had risen in pitch, and Cade took a step toward her. "Tell me he didn't really touch you."

She watched the pulse in his neck grow faster and his jaw set. "What would it matter?"

"Olivia, I know my own father took a swing at the man over it."

This time she had to smile, though it wasn't worth rejoicing in, but she remembered it so well. "Oh, he didn't take a swing, he nailed the jerk."

"He actually hit him?"

"Over and over." She could still see her stepfather bent over in pain. "He'd attacked me…"

"Olivia," he reached for her. "You never told me that."

"You didn't talk to me anymore, remember?"

Cade nodded and stepped back.

"It wasn't the first time. He'd tried a few times, and I'd always managed to get out of it." She turned and moved toward the couch, but he'd covered it in boxes so she just stood there, her back to him. "That last time he'd left a mark and your father saw it. The accusations went back and forth. He accused your father of inappropriate things, and your father threatened to kill him if he touched me again."

"And then he hit him?"

Olivia nodded, and she let the smile land large on her lips. "Oh, yeah. He hit him."

Cade shook his head. "I can't even imagine."

"He took care of me as if I were one of his own."

"He used to race over when you were small and your mother would leave you asleep in the house alone. We could hear you scream in your sleep, and he never knew who your mom had in the house with you."

The smile was gone and Olivia moved to him. "I screamed in my sleep?"

"Yeah. You had nightmares or something."

She let out a breath. "I didn't know that. But that explains a lot." She looked up at him and his eyes were narrowed. "Gage does that."

"I've never heard him scream."

"When you're around, he doesn't. He's comfortable with you."

That was a truth that hurt her.

She gripped her car keys in her hand tightly. "I think we should talk."

He stood there in front of her with his hands on his hips. He looked at his watch. "Where is Gage?"

"He's with my mom."

He shifted his eyes and shook his head disapprovingly. "Let's go get him."

Cade had a lot to sort out in his mind. He'd come back to Aspen Creek to close up his father's life,; he'd never in his wildest dreams imagined he'd fall in love.

He'd tried to work it out in his head. It was just coming home and she was a familiar face. No, that wasn't the truth and he knew it.

Olivia had been a stranger for years. Meeting her now had proved that.

He'd not only fallen in love with her, but then there was Gage. His heart ached at the thought that he might never see him again.

Love had been everywhere in that stupid, little town and Cade wanted to ignore it. He loved the feel of the mountain air during the summer nights. It wasn't too hot, and it was just cool enough to keep you comfortable while you slept. He loved the sound of Aspen Creek as it flowed under the Rose Bridge and the slow mornings in town.

Before school would start in the fall, the echo of the marching band filled the valley and the grunts from the football players practicing on the field did the same.

He'd been on the phone with Ashley about sixty times since he'd left his aunt's house in Vegas. Nothing and no one in Green Bay needed him or had even noticed he'd been gone. But the woman and boy in Aspen Creek seemed to be keeping his time, mind, and heart occupied.

Ashley said the house was fine and beer was plentiful. The view of Lake Michigan was beautiful and his ugly mug would only ruin it. That had made him laugh.

Olivia parked the car in front of the motel and turned off the engine. "I'll be right back."

He reached for her and touched her arm. "I want to go in with you."

She agreed with a nod.

By the look on Celeste Baker's face, the day had been a hard one. Cade wasn't sure what Olivia had been thinking, leaving her son with her mother all day. It didn't sound like a good idea to him.

Gage was balanced on her hip. His face and hands were sticky and dirty, and his cheeks were tear stained.

The moment he saw his mother, he leapt for her.

"Gage, it's okay. Mom, what happened to him?"

Celeste lifted her hands in the air. "He's a handful, this one." She looked past Olivia and her stare bore right into Cade. "Nice to see you, Cade."

The words were courteous, but the tone was much different.

"Ms. Baker." Gage looked over his mother's shoulder and saw him. He reached out and Cade took him from Olivia. "Hey, big guy, you look like you had a busy day."

Gage rested his head on Cade's shoulder and the ache he'd felt in his chest for the past week eased.

"Mom, let's go inside and get his things." Olivia started for the door.

"Actually, why don't you take Gage, get him cleaned up, and let me talk to Cade."

Olivia shot him a look, and he nodded as he handed Gage back to her.

Celeste watched her daughter go back into the room and then turned her eyes to him. "Let's walk down to the end there and get me some ice."

Cade walked with her. He didn't remember her looking so old, but such a hateful life would cause anyone to look years older.

"I met up with your aunt in Las Vegas. She's doing well," she said.

What a pair of interesting women, he thought. Nothing good would, or did, ever come from the two of them together. "I've seen her recently."

"I'm curious. What was my daughter doing with your father? Seems odd to me that he left her everything and cut you out completely."

Cade clenched his jaw. "I don't see where that is anyone's business but my father's and Olivia's."

She nodded. "Looks like my grandson has already taken to you. I suppose that's good since he looks just like you."

Cade looked back toward the room. Olivia was carrying Gage to the car. "Do you think so?"

She gave a small groan. "I'm sure it didn't escape you." She narrowed her eyes on him. "Is he your kid?"

Cade contemplated his answer. Gage certainly could be his son, and the thought sparked something in him. But he assumed she'd also seen the birth certificate if she knew about the contents of the will. "You don't know who his father is?"

Celeste shrugged her shoulder and stopped as they approached the ice machine. She took a plastic bucket from atop the machine and held it under the dispenser.

"Your aunt had some papers that told us who his daddy was."

"And you think that's how it is?"

She shifted a glance to him. "I think that's how it's been for years. Even my ex-husband had words with him over it."

The mention of her ex-husband had the heat rising under his collar. The man was a horrible man who had nearly violated Olivia on more than one occasion, and Celeste had blamed her for it. "If I remember correctly, the words were had by my father about your ex-husband laying hands on her, not my father."

"You didn't bother to come around for the past decade, but you'll defend him?"

He looked back at Olivia as she strapped Gage in. "Yes, I'd defend my father and I hope Gage will too, someday."

"I know that look in your eye. You're thinking of snatching him up as if he were your own. Give him a name. Step in as the heroic daddy."

Of course he'd thought that. That's what happened when you fell in love with a mother and her child. "He *is* mine." And, in his heart, he felt that.

Celeste's eyes narrowed as though he'd completely confused her, but he found humor in that. As far as he was concerned now, no one else was left for Gage. And no matter what happened between him and Olivia, if Gage was in fact his father's son, he'd take care of him forever.

"My aunt told me you'd stopped by. Just so you know, Olivia is protesting the will. She doesn't want what was left to her, and she plans to pay me back the money my father lent her."

"That sounds like her. Always too reasonable for her own good."

"You're right. That sounds like her."

Celeste let out a sigh and looked out over the parking lot. "This town hasn't gotten any better, has it? It's still a dump."

"I think that is the charm of it."

She started back toward her room, and he walked with her. "You know, I think I'm having second thoughts about settling down here. She's doing fine without me. Maybe I'll come back around Christmas."

"I think she'd like that."

Celeste stopped before they'd reached her room. "I don't know why you'd want to take on your father's mess, but she's always had a soft spot for you."

"I'm counting on that."

"You'll be reconsidering it, I'm sure."

Celeste gave a wave to Olivia, who was already sitting behind the wheel of the car, and then closed herself back into her motel room. Cade was sure that was the last they'd see of her for a while.

He opened the passenger door and climbed into the car.

He looked at Olivia who sat there gripping the steering wheel, her eyes wide open and full of fear.

"She's here to see what she can get her hands on, isn't she?"

"I think she'd considered it," Cade said as he turned and looked at the sleepy boy in the back seat. "I told her you planned to contest the will. She's not interested in staying if you're not profiting."

A tear slid down her cheek. "How is it possible I was born to that woman?"

"We don't get to choose who we are born to, but we can choose the families we keep." She turned her head and looked at him. He might have said too much.

Olivia pulled up in front of his house. The painters were cleaning up, and he was glad to know they'd be gone.

"I'm going to pay these guys and get some things together. I'll be over in a bit."

He watched her face tense. "Are you sure?"

He shook his head. "I'm so confused right now that I can't even wrap my head around what I'm feeling. But I know I want to spend the night with both of you. I need that." He reached over and touched her cheek. "Besides, you and I still need to talk."

Olivia nodded and looked at Gage, who rubbed his eyes. "I'll get him settled then."

"I'll bring something for dinner." He climbed out of the car and headed into the house.

Cade paid the painters and packed a bag for the night. It might have been the dumbest idea in the world, but the need to spend one more night with Olivia was keeping him from thinking straight.

He dropped his bag on the couch and looked down at the box he'd brought up from the basement. It had Gage's name on it.

He hadn't thought too much about it at first, but when he'd looked at the note that was taped to it, he knew he had to give it to him. But it wasn't his place to open it. He wasn't like his aunt or Olivia's mother. At least he wasn't going to be, no matter how much he wanted to know what was in the box. After all, he'd already seen the birth certificate.

As he turned off the lights, his cell phone rang.

"Ashley, what's up?"

"Are you ever coming back? This place is getting lonely."

"I'm sure you're keeping enough company."

"You're right. But seriously, you've had a few phone calls I think you should return."

Cade picked up his bag and the box, and with his phone balanced on his shoulder, he headed out to his car. "Who needs me now?"

"The city of Green Bay, that's who. Seems like there's a coaching position opening up."

Cade stopped on the front porch. "Are you kidding me?"

"Really, would I kid you about money?"

"Nope." He pulled the front door closed and continued down the steps. "So, what's the deal?"

"You get your butt home and talk to these people. C'mon, this house needs a housekeeper. I'm tired of cleaning."

"I'm sure it's a wreck."

"You know me."

And he did, all too well. "Okay, text me the information and I'll make the call in the morning."

"In the morning? Are you serious? I'd get your butt back into that tiny, toy car of yours and get back here."

"Listen, my dad seems to have left me a bigger mess than I'd thought."

"Hmmm, yeah, you're getting soft on me. What did they do, give you a sign?"

Cade chuckled. "Yeah."

"Don't mess this up. Get back here as fast as you can."

"I'll be there tomorrow."

"That's more like it."

Cade loaded the box into the passenger seat, climbed into the driver's seat, and started toward Olivia's. Now there was more to think about. Since the moment he'd caught that football and ended his career, he had wondered what was next. A coaching position was exactly what he wanted. Would Olivia move to Wisconsin? Did he want her to?

Chapter Eleven

It was almost dark when Olivia opened her eyes, and she realized that when she'd sat down to rock with Gage, she too had fallen asleep.

She carried Gage into his room and set him in his crib. They were both exhausted, and she wished she'd listened to her gut and not taken him to spend the day with her mother.

But even more upsetting was the fact that Cade hadn't returned.

Things hadn't gone as she'd wanted them to. Why did she think he'd want them in his life? No one else had ever wanted her.

No one, but… she heard the knocking on the door and she lifted her head.

Olivia hurried through the house and sucked in a breath when she saw Cade standing on the doorstep with a large box in his arms. He had come back.

"Sorry, I was laying Gage down." She opened the door.

Cade walked in and set the box on the floor. "He didn't fall asleep right away?"

"We both did." She closed the door and looked up at the man who was wreaking havoc with her heart. "I thought you'd be here a long time ago."

"Yeah. Needed to drive around—clear my head." He ran his hand over the back of his neck. "I ran into Coach Cal. Things around here have changed a lot. You don't have anything to drink, do you? Non kid friendly."

Olivia studied him for a moment, taking in all the nonsense he seemed to be talking, and nodded. She walked toward the kitchen with him close behind. She opened the cabinet above the refrigerator and then turned to grab a chair.

Cade rested his hand on hers. "I'll get it."

He pulled down the bottle of whiskey and blew the dust from it. "Guess you don't drink this very often."

"I have some very hefty responsibilities." She opened a cupboard door and reached for a glass.

Cade took it from her and poured in no more than a swallow. He lifted it to his lips and drank it down.

"That stuff was always bad."

"What has you so worked up that you're drinking?"

"You."

Olivia pulled the bottle from his hand and set it on the counter. "I will not have another man tell me I cause him so much pain that he has to drink it away."

Cade's eyes opened wide. "I didn't mean it like that."

"You're no different than…" She felt the anger and the sob that lodged in her throat fight for their escape. "Where have you been? You said you'd be right here? You were having second thoughts, right?"

"You're not making any of this easy."

"Nothing in this life is easy, Cade."

He shook his head and his lips tightened. "Let's just get this out in the open." He pulled a piece of paper out of his pocket and handed it to her. "You owe me an explanation."

She'd rather have pushed him out the door than to have him speak to her like that, but she took the paper from his hand and opened it. There was no reason for the tears not to fall now.

Cade took a step closer to her. "Gage is my brother. That is why he's comfortable around me and why he looks just like me."

"No. No, you don't understand."

"What's to understand, Olivia? Right there," he pointed to the paper, "it lists my dad as the father of your baby. How can you even deny that? And that box," he pointed toward the door, "was for Gage. My dad left him a letter telling Gage it was for him so he'd feel closer to his dad."

"Cade…"

"And the picture in the bedroom. He was there when that precious boy took his first breath."

Olivia nodded, and the sobs shook her body. "He held my hand the entire time."

Cade grabbed her shoulders, and she was forced to look up at him. "Then, damn it, just tell me the truth. I'll take care of him. No matter what happens to us, I'll help take care of Gage." He loosened his grip. "At this point, he's just as much my responsibility."

The sobs stopped, and the anger pushed through. Olivia pushed back from him. "Your responsibility? No one asked you to take care of anyone."

"I just want him to be better off than we were."

"He has a loving mother and that will take care of everything."

Cade stepped back. "I can't believe he didn't even marry you or give your son his name."

"You're not listening to me, are you?" She shoved the paper at him. "Go open the box, Cade. Take your time, but then you'll know. You'll know who Gage's father is, and then you can decide how you feel about it."

She walked to the back door and pushed it open. The air was thick and hot, and even the mountain breeze didn't help to cool her off.

How had it come to this? How had she gotten so deep with him?

The back door opened, and she felt Cade's presence. She lifted her head, but didn't turn to look at him. Instead she closed her eyes.

He took her hand and held it palm up. Cade laid something metal in her palm and closed her hand around it.

He moved in close to her, and she could feel his breath on her cheek. "Conner is Gage's father?"

Again, the sobs moved in, and when she opened her eyes, she saw his Marine tags in her hand.

There were no words. She could only nod.

She saw his shoulders drop, and he pulled her in close to him. "Why is my father's name on the birth certificate?"

"Because he was a stubborn, old man."

Cade laughed. "Yes, he was."

She pulled back and looked at the pieces of metal in her hand. She ran her thumb over Conner's name. "When Gage was born, he wanted me to put Conner's name on the certificate. I disagreed. He didn't want the baby. He shouldn't get to have his name on there, dead or alive. So when I asked your dad to mail the forms for me, he took them and when I got the certificate back, his name had been added."

"Why would he do that?"

Olivia looked up at him. "How else could he have given Gage everything in his will?"

Cade walked across the porch to an old, plastic chair against the wall. "He was setting him up?"

"That would be my guess. He knew I'd have to struggle for everything. And I'm very sure he knew he wouldn't be around for much longer. That was why he made me leave his house and lent me the money for this house."

"Gave you the money."

She gritted her teeth. "I said I'd pay you back."

Cade shook his head. "No. I meant that sincerely. I want you to keep it. If Gage meant that much to my dad then he should have a good home to live in."

He reached his hand up to her and she took it. Cade pulled her to him until she sat on his lap. "Why didn't Conner want the baby?"

Olivia sucked in a breath. "Would you think it was a good idea to have a child if the only upbringing you knew was the torture he lived through?"

"No."

"Well that was all he could think about. And then there was Iraq."

Cade looked up at her, his eyes narrowed. "What happened to him?"

"He watched as an entire family was murdered."

"Olivia, no."

She nodded and wiped the tears which had begun to fall again from her cheeks. "They shot the father and son, raped the mother and older daughter and then shot them. But there was a baby…"

She couldn't say it. She knew she didn't have to. "That family's sacrifice and Conner not giving up his position saved nearly two hundred lives."

She let out a breath, trying to calm her rattled nerves. "They were trying to pull civilians out of harm's way, trying to get them aide. Eventually their cover was blown. Some of the civilians were shot, but they got all the men who had murdered the family. But not before they shot Conner."

"I didn't know he'd been shot."

Olivia pointed to her shoulder. "It was something fixable, but what it did to him on the inside… Cade, you can't repair that."

"Why did he kill himself?"

"He couldn't let go of what he'd seen." She stood from his lap and paced the porch. "Between the abuses he endured when he was young and what he saw as an adult, it took over. He began to drink heavily, and then when you turned him away…" She stopped. She hadn't meant to include that.

Cade stood quickly and then caught the chair to balance him. "Don't blame his death on me."

"I'm not." She held up a defensive hand. "He was crushed Cade. He looked up to you. He always had."

Cade scrubbed his hands over his face. "And I let him down, just like I let everyone else down."

Olivia moved to him and put her hands on his chest. "Don't think that way. You couldn't have done what you've done if you stayed here or kept it close to your heart."

"I should have taken care of dad and Conner. And you."

She stepped back. "I did fine on my own."

"Yes, you did." He reached for her again. "I just don't understand how you ended up with Conner."

She smiled. "Conner was always one step behind you, but sometimes so were the rest of us." She walked to the edge of the porch and rested against the railing. "After I moved and you started playing football in junior high school, Conner and I found ourselves," she considered for a moment, "outcast together. Our friendship grew stronger, but he was still distant."

"So Conner was always your boyfriend when I became the enemy?"

"He was there when I needed him."

Cade nodded. "I'm sorry I was so hurtful to you both back then. I had no reason to be."

"I won't say it's okay or I even forgive you, but I'm willing to give you a chance."

His shoulders dropped. "I can't stay."

Olivia crossed her arms over her chest and watched him as he tucked his thumbs into the front pockets of his jeans. "I suppose I expected that."

"But," he reached his hand to her cheek and held it there caressing it with his thumb, "you could come with me."

That statement shocked her to the very core. "Back to Green Bay?"

"Yes." He moved to her and took her in his arms. "I'm confused right now. I came home to clean out my father's life. I didn't expect to have missed it—and everyone. But I have some opportunities. I just…" He stopped and huffed out a breath. "Marry me."

Olivia felt the blood drain from her head. She was sure she could pass out right in his arms. Had Cade Carter actually just asked her to marry him?

There wasn't much time to think. There was only one answer when it came to his marriage proposal.

Chapter Twelve

Cade hadn't meant to slam the door or wake Gage as he stormed out of the house, but he was mad. After everything they'd been through in the past week, she'd turned him down flat.

He sped out of the valley and headed back to Wisconsin in the dark. This time he wasn't sure he'd ever come back.

The air in the little car grew thick. He rolled down the windows just to breathe, but all of his emotions were stuck in his chest. There was no denying it, he was heartbroken.

He drove until he made it to Denver in the dark and deep wee hours of the morning. He took the exit to Pena Boulevard and headed toward the airport. There was no way he was going to make it back to Green Bay by tomorrow without killing himself or someone else on the road. He'd fly out, and he'd figure out his car later.

The wait for a flight was long, but he had to admit watching the sun rise over the plains of Colorado was something he'd long missed.

He'd called Ashley four times from the airport, but there was no answer. No doubt out on the lake in *his boat,* drinking *his beer,* and probably wrecking *his house.* Funny, none of that mattered when he was with Olivia.

The taxi pulled up to the gates in front of his house. The house that football built. His dungeon to live out his days after football took it all away. There was the slightest bit of regret that he'd left Olivia the way he had only to return to take a position he hadn't been offered yet.

He ran his hand over his head and then wiped his weary eyes. When would he learn that the world didn't revolve around him? Who did he think he was?

There was a dull ache in his chest. His father had cared for him all his life, and yet he'd been the kind of son who thought he was smothering him. But that was tough love. It wasn't like Conner's house where his mother beat him until he couldn't go to school. Where it was better to hide in the tree house with booze you found when you were thirteen and get drunk so you'd pass out and not have to go home.

The dull ache sharpened. What if his mother had stayed in Aspen Creek and tried to be a mother? Would he have hated her? Would she have been any different than Celeste Baker? He doubted it. He would have been just like Olivia, always alone and wondering when her mother would be home and with whom.

A bead of sweat formed on his brow as he punched in the code for the gate, and the taxi drove through.

What would Gage think of his father?

Conner wasn't a bad kid, really. And, after all, he'd fought for his country. What had Cade done? Upped the ratings on Monday night? Sure, he'd done his volunteer work. That was part of his contract. He'd made his appearances and played until it nearly killed him, but he had never saved a life. Conner had saved many.

The taxi driver pulled to a stop in front of the house and turned to him. Cade pulled his wallet from his pocket and paid the hefty tab.

He inched out of the taxi. His entire body hurt, but his leg was the worst. It was so stiff he could hardly set it on the ground and limp to the front door.

There was no surprise that when he put his hand on the doorknob, the door pushed open. Cade let out a very slow and controlled breath.

Already he could hear music coming from the back of the house. If Ashley had a real job…he shook the thought from his head.

He'd been thinking about adopting Gage. He'd forgotten he had another child living in his own home. A grown one who could make the biggest messes, which he'd noted as he walked through the house.

"You are the biggest pig I have ever met."

Ashley looked up at him and gave him a deep grunt. "Ya made it. GM will be plenty happy to see you."

Cade took a step further out onto the porch. "You have a beer in that cooler that you could spare?"

"Help yourself."

He did just that and sat down in the adjacent lounge chair. Cade looked over at the chair next to him. "Are you seriously sunbathing in your Speedo and cowboy boots?"

The enormous man next to him turned his head and grinned. "The ladies love me."

And that they did. Ashley Wilkie was the most unique man Cade Carter had ever known. The uniqueness started with the name. His mother was so fanatical about *Gone with the Wind* that she named all of her children after the four main characters. It was Ashley's misfortune not to be the first boy or not to have been a girl. But he'd made the most of it. His mother had even gone so far as to marry a man whose name resembled Wilkes. Mrs. Wilkie was fair skinned and blonde. Mr. Wilkie was a tall, black man from deep in Louisiana, but he knew his football. He took his son and trained him the best he could. It landed Ashley Wilkie a very nice football contract in the end, and Cade Carter owed Ashley Wilkie everything.

Ashley Wilkie was a full six foot four, which towered over Cade's six foot. It had never slowed him down any. He had blue eyes and caramel colored skin. Ashley was never in need of female company. He always had plenty and was willing to share. Cade thought it was interesting that he didn't even care to ask where all the women were. There was only one woman he wanted and he'd crushed her heart—again.

Ashley lifted his glasses and glanced at Cade. "You look like shit."

"I knew you could comfort me like no one else."

Ashley laughed and relaxed back into his chair. "You need a drink or four, a dip in the pool, and I have some very nice, young ladies coming over later. I'll let you have your pick."

"I don't think so," he said as he pulled from his beer.

This time, Ashley sat up on the chair. "You don't think so? When did Cade Carter ever turn down a woman?"

Cade chuckled. "When he realized he just walked out on the woman he loved."

That had Ashley up and out of his seat. The gold necklace swayed on his bare chest as he looked down at Cade. "You what? I sent you home to pay your respects to your father, not to fall in love with some small town honey."

"It gets worse. She has a son."

"Damn! I thought I taught you better than this."

Cade smiled and sipped his beer again. He needed a dose of Ashley's abuse to feel better.

"You love her?"

"Asked her to marry me."

"Fool. And she has a kid?"

"Yep. I thought he was my father's son, but it turns out he's my cousin."

Ashley shook his head. "You have confused the hell out of me. I didn't think you Westerners cross-contaminated the gene pool like that." He let out another grunt. "There is pizza in the fridge. Go get us some. I'm going to cool off in the pool." He shook his head. "You *are* a fool."

Cade chuckled as he walked back into the house. He was a fool. But now what was he going to do about it?

He looked around the enormous kitchen in the house that football had provided him with. There had been hundreds of parties there, friends were many, and the women had been plentiful. And yet, the thought of macaroni and cheese in his father's small and dingy kitchen warmed him to the core.

His cell phone rang in his pocket, and he pulled it out quickly hoping it was Olivia on the other end. But it wasn't. He shouldn't have been disappointed to find the name of the team's general manager on the caller ID, but he couldn't help it. It was a letdown.

Cade cleared his throat and reminded himself that she'd turned down his proposal. It was time to answer this call and accept his new position in life—washed up football player with a new coaching title.

Olivia had cleaned every surface in her house. She had pushed Gage in the stroller through town and back three times in two days and had nearly worn a hole in the bottom of her shoe. But it was the hole in her heart she was most worried about.

What had she been thinking to have gone to bed with Cade—to have lost her heart to him again? Oh, she couldn't have been more foolish. The man was still the boy, and that would never change. Just as she was still the girl who needed to forget her foolish dreams of Cade Carter loving her and move on with her life.

It had been an emotional couple of weeks. That had to be why she let things get to the point where she was now longing for him and hating him at the same time. She'd needed to fill a void in her heart, and it was horrible to think she could fill it with Cade.

Guilt ripped through her. What would Austin have thought if he knew things would have happened as they had with her and Cade?

Austin. Why was she even thinking of Cade at all? She should be focused on Austin.

How could she forget that moment when Austin clenched his chest, and she caught him as he fell? There had been no time to say goodbye. He was gone before they hit the floor.

He'd been the only man to take care of her, and she hated that everyone made it into something that it wasn't. Her mother hadn't given her a father, and her stepfather had only abused her. Austin had always protected her from the world, even years later when her stepfather had come after her. Only that time, she'd also fallen in with Conner.

She rubbed the tension from her forehead.

So much had happened that fall when Conner happened into her life—when Austin had tucked her away in Grand Junction again after her ex-stepfather came looking for her. She'd never considered that maybe Conner was hiding too, and she was the connection to his past, yet a safe friend.

Her entire life he'd just been Cade's cousin—the quiet one—the sad one—the follower. It seemed as though Conner Carter was always in trouble, but he just had the knack of being in the wrong place at the wrong time—always.

Olivia lifted her hand to her mouth. How had she ever let it get so far as to have an affair with him?

It was brief.

It was sad.

It was stupid.

It gave her the one thing in her life that she now knew she could never live without. She had Gage.

Olivia snapped her head up when she heard the buzzer on the dryer, and she hurried to take the clothes out. She was sure she'd washed that load twice, but with her head in the clouds, she supposed it didn't matter.

She folded a towel and then refolded it. Even the simple things were beyond her now. Then she pulled the T-shirt she'd worn home from Cade's house out of the dryer and stood there staring at it.

Oklahoma University, the shirt read. Cade had taken that scholarship and ridden it all the way to the pros, never once looking back and revisiting the man, or the community, which had given him the chance to become the MVP, Cade Carter.

Olivia folded the shirt and set it on the dryer. She needed to return it—to where? Oh, he wasn't coming back. When was she going to get that through her skull? It was her and Gage again. Conner had turned his back on them, Austin had left them, and now Cade. Damn it if she wasn't going to raise *her* Carter man right!

She could hear Gage stirring in his bedroom. Nap time was over, and she needed to stifle her mood. It didn't matter that Cade was gone. It was a momentary lapse of judgment, and Gage wouldn't remember him in time. She was going to focus on one day at a time. Friday was the Fourth of July and the Aspen Creek Fourth Festival. She didn't have to work, and she could leave all her worries behind her and spoil her son in a tradition she'd missed for years. And that night, she'd lay down a blanket in the center of town, and with the only man she needed, her son, she'd watch the fireworks light up the sky. It would be her celebration—her new beginning.

Olivia opened the door to Gage's room, and he was standing in his crib grinning at her.

"Mama!" He held his arms out to her.

"Hey, big guy." She lifted him from the crib and held him tight to her.

Gage took her face in his hands and pushed his forehead to hers. She loved when he cuddled and did silly things.

"Dade!"

Olivia felt the ache in her chest immediately. Damn Cade Carter to hell. He'd promised not to break Gage's heart. If she ever saw him again, he'd pay.

Chapter Thirteen

Cade had spent all of Monday and Tuesday at the corporate headquarters talking job offers. However, he wasn't sure he'd heard one. They needed an assistant to the GM. They needed someone to help with special teams. What he was hearing was they needed a mascot to make them look good, and he seemed to be the guy for the job.

He sat poolside with his feet dangling in the water, listening to the boats out in the bay. The house, the cars, the money, and the fame left him empty inside. Women had come and gone for years, friends were a dime a dozen, but old tree houses withstood the test of time.

He didn't remember catching the ball, which won the championship that year, or crashing to the ground and nearly losing his life, but he did remember the moment his lips touched Olivia's for the first time, so many years ago.

Memories flooded back at him quickly. She'd been the one to shove him into Aspen Creek, and she'd been there, with Conner, to pull him out. Olivia had knocked the first beer out of his hand at age eleven, and had been the one who got caught stealing her mother's cigarettes for him, too.

He looked out over the bay. Where he sat was where most people wanted to be. Right in the middle of luxury and riches, but he wasn't happy.

There was a dusty couch in a dark house, down the stairs from a room full of trophies, where he thought heaven on earth might be. No, that was only another place where good memories enveloped him and he'd walked away from. Heaven on earth was wrapped in Olivia's arms. It was the way Gage looked up at him and called him Dade. It was being *home*.

Did it matter that the Carter eyes that stared up at him were because of Conner? Did Olivia ever love Conner as much as Cade loved her?

He inched away from the pool. His mind was so scattered that if he got any closer to the water he might drown.

He loved her.

He loved them both.

What the hell was he doing in Green Bay, Wisconsin when his family was in Aspen Creek, Colorado?

"Hey," Ashley called from the house. "You have a phone call."

"Take a message."

"Get your ass in here. This one is a coaching position. You ain't gonna want to pass this up."

Olivia picked out an outfit for Gage. A pair of blue shorts and a red T-shirt with a flag on it was very appropriate for the Fourth of July.

She turned toward the crib to dress him, and he'd put the blanket over his head.

"Are you hiding?" She reached to peek under it, and he slapped at her.

"Dade."

Olivia set her jaw. "Cade isn't here. Let's get dressed and go have fun at the park today."

"Dade!"

Oh, there had been times when she'd grown frustrated with her son before. What parent hadn't? But this time, she was feeling the sting of anger.

"Gage Baker, let's get dressed and go to town. No more talk of Dade…I mean Cade."

For the next twenty minutes, she struggled with the strong-minded toddler. By the time she'd gotten his arms through the sleeves of the T-shirt, her hair had fallen into her eyes and a bead of sweat rolled down the back of her neck. The room was hot, her nerves were shot, and she thought she just might get sick.

Gage reached his arms up to her as if he'd noticed she needed him. She pulled him in close and held tight. He was all she had. Cade Carter wasn't about to ruin that.

She packed them a picnic while Gage sat on the floor with his cars. When she was done, she carried it to the front door and turned to see Gage holding an old teddy bear.

"Where did you get that?"

Gage turned and pointed. "Box."

The bear was Conner's, and she remembered it well. Tears burned her eyes and quickly rolled down her cheeks.

She'd tried to forget the box Cade had brought over. She hadn't looked inside, and she hadn't wanted to. Everything was too raw, and her emotions were unstable.

Olivia sat down, right in the middle of the floor.

Gage hurried to her and handed her the bear, then he slid into her lap.

She kissed the top of his head. "That was your daddy's bear." Austin had been gracious enough to think ahead and build memories of Gage's father for him. The least she could do was share them.

"Dade."

She wrapped her arms around him tighter. He didn't understand now, but in time, he would.

The park was full of people, some from town, others were tourists. Aspen Creek knew how to throw a party, and the people came every year for the celebration.

Olivia left the cooler with the picnic in the car and walked toward the tent where she saw Kat working the bake sale.

"Well, look at that big boy," Kat hollered, and Gage buried his face into Olivia's neck. "I can't believe how much he's grown."

"Already it's going so fast."

"Mine were born, and then they were gone."

Olivia wasn't sure that was comforting.

Kat scanned over the crowd. "No, Cade? I thought he was back."

Olivia forced a smile on her face and shook her head, but at the mention of his name, Gage's head had popped up.

"Dade."

The wide eyes of Kat McCormik had trouble brewing in them. "Dade? Isn't that cute? Do you suppose that's his way of saying dad?"

"I sure hope so." The voice resonated behind Olivia, and she spun around.

Limping toward her was Cade.

Gage's arms reached for him and Cade took him, giving him an enormous squeeze. "Hey, buddy, I missed you."

Gage rested his head on Cade's shoulder, and Cade kissed the top of his head.

Olivia's body tensed and began to shake. "What are you doing here?"

"I have a house here, remember?"

"You left."

"You said you wouldn't marry me."

Olivia let out a frustrated grunt as he moved in closer to her. She didn't like the scene he was making, especially with Kat standing so close. "Cade, give me Gage."

"Have you changed your mind yet?"

"About what?"

He reached for her, resting his hand on her cheek. "Marrying me."

"I am very sure you hit your head harder than you think you did on that field. It's just taken two years for you to lose your mind."

"I lost my mind the day you came into my life in the flower-print sundress when you were six."

She heard the gasp from Kat and pulled away from Cade.

"Maybe Gage and I should go."

Cade looked at Gage and shook his head. "I really think this kiddo needs a new stuffed animal." Gage sat straight up and laughed. "Yep, let's go." He turned to Olivia. "Comin'?"

What choice did she have? Obviously Gage was happy with him. She'd let him spoil her son.

Cade had hoped that the festivities would relax Olivia and they could work some things out. He wasn't going to tell her about the coaching position he'd taken until he was sure she would accept him back.

He understood, deep inside of him, that she still might continue to say no to his marriage proposal, but he wasn't about to leave Gage. After all, Gage was the only family he had left.

He looked to his side, and the woman he loved walked quietly beside them. "Are you okay?"

"Fine."

"I've always been told when a woman says fine, it's not."

She dropped her shoulders and looked up at him. "I'm hot. I'm hungry. I'm cranky. I'm tired. And I just don't feel good. Add that to you just showing up and Gage's attachment to you, I think my head is just might explode."

Cade stopped walking. "I don't want to hurt you."

"I know. But it's hard when I've spent so much time being mad at you…"

"You have to stop."

She fisted her hands on her hips. "Why? Because you come back and ask me to marry you?"

It did sound bad when she said it. "It's not going to be like that anymore."

He could see her consider it by the way she dropped her eyes, but the next voice he heard calling his name had sent Olivia's shoulders back, her jaw had set, and now her knuckles were white.

Cade turned to see Patsy Woods walking his way.

Of all the people in the world to interrupt their conversation, she had to be the worst.

"Oh-my-God! You are here. Parker said you were in town, but I didn't believe him."

She moved past Olivia without a thought and kissed him right on the lips. Gage shifted in his arms. Even he knew she was trouble.

"Look at this. You have a little boy. Oh, he is precious! He has your eyes and looks just like you. Lucky little man."

He realized he hadn't even had a moment to talk, but he wasn't going to correct her on Gage's paternity. No need. Gage was his, as far as he was concerned. He was a Carter, and it was time he got the recognition of being one.

"So you're married? I know you're not playing football anymore. I saw that play when you got hurt. Knocked you out cold. So where is his mama?"

Cade watched as Olivia stepped between them. "I'm his mother, Patsy."

Patsy looked her over from head to toe and shook her head. "Do I know you?"

"Oh, you know me. Olivia Baker."

Patsy actually gasped aloud, but with her well-manicured hand lifted to her lips, she did all she could to compose herself while looking at Olivia.

"You sure have changed."

"I'll bet I have."

"Parker always did have a thing for you, though I don't know what he ever saw in you before." Patsy readjusted her purse on her shoulder. "You must have lost a hundred pounds and had a whole makeover. And now you two…" She wagged a finger between them. "I never saw that coming, especially after all the nights you and I spent together."

Cade felt the anger begin to coarse though his veins, just as it did the night he threw Buck through the jukebox. "Patsy…"

"We had a good thing, didn't we? Remember the backseat of my car, down by the creek?"

Olivia turned to him, her eyes full of fury. She pulled Gage from his arms and walked away. He certainly didn't blame her.

"Nice to see you, Patsy." He turned, but she caught his arm.

"Really? You and Baker? C'mon, what's the real story? You wouldn't have felt her up if she paid you. Now you have a kid?" She shook her head. "She was white trash. How'd you make a woman out of her that you'd want to keep?"

He could see Olivia heading to the parking lot.

Cade wondered at that moment what he'd ever seen in Patsy Woods. How many tumbles had they taken? How many lies had he told to be with her? It was her promise of one more time that had him driving away from his father for the last time.

Guilt riddled him, and he thought his heart might explode as he watched Gage struggle to sit in the car as Olivia buckled him in.

She deserved better than the man he'd been. Standing so close to Patsy Woods, he could feel the person he was nearly ooze away. It wasn't what he wanted anymore. No more women. No more booze or late nights. He wanted the woman he loved and the child with his eyes.

"Ya know, Patsy, all those years ago I was wrong. I should have been sitting on that porch swing or been up in that tree with Olivia when I was off *feeling you up*. It should have been her with me that last night in town, not you." He nodded. "I was an idiot. But ya know what? I'm never going to make that mistake again."

He adjusted his sunglasses. "I'll see you around. You're not worth my time."

Cade had driven straight to Olivia's house, but she wasn't there. That was a cause for alarm because where did she have that she could go? Her home and her son were all she had.

But as he stood on her front porch looking in the window, he saw the box he'd brought, still on the floor where he'd sat it. He knew exactly where she was.

Ten minutes later, he found her sitting on the ground next to his father's grave.

He parked his car in the lot and eased out of the confined seat. Gage had looked up at him, but he didn't run to him. He sat in his mother's lap as if he knew she needed the comfort of him near.

"Olivia, I'm sorry for all that. I owe you years of apologies."

Her cheeks were streaked with tears, and she shook her head at him. "I wasn't worth anyone's time back then. My mother didn't want me. You didn't want me. My stepfather only wanted…" She wiped at her eyes. "The only two people who ever treated me kindly are right here. Buried in the ground. And I'm still here facing the same people they tried to protect me from."

"I don't want to be one of those people who hurt you anymore. If the Carter men were the ones in your life that made sense then I should be in your life."

"You were the one I wanted, and you were the one who didn't care."

"That's not true." He moved to her and tried to kneel down, but his knee wouldn't bend. Damn it! "Olivia, stand up so I can talk to you."

"I don't want to talk to you anymore. You're causing me so much pain just being here."

"You need me here."

She shifted her jaw in the air. "I've never needed anyone."

"Listen, Gage is my family. I deserve to be with him even if you hate me."

The tears started again and that cut him deep. How was it he could always make her cry?

"My problem is that I don't hate you. I never did hate you and that drove me in the wrong direction—into the arms of the wrong Carter man."

"Then let me be the one to love you."

"I don't think you can."

The air squeezed in his lungs. She was right. When had he ever loved anyone but himself?

"Come back to the house with me. I have things I want to talk about."

"Aspen Creek is my home. I'm not moving."

"And I'm not going to ask you to move." He reached down to her and helped her from the ground. "Hear me out. And after, if you feel the need, you can kick me out."

She focused on him for a moment and then a smile formed on her lips. "I do think I hate you."

"I don't blame you."

This time Gage reached up for him, and he pulled him into his arms and walked back to the parking lot with his arms around both the people he wanted to love the most. Now he had to figure out how to tell her about his plans. That could seriously disrupt the progress he hoped he was making.

Chapter Fourteen

Gage had fallen asleep on the ride down from the cemetery, and Olivia was glad. She needed the ten minute drive to think about what she was going to do.

She'd waited her whole life for Cade Carter, and now he was begging for her. But Patsy had certainly raised some red flags. After all, she and Cade were different.

There was a lot to consider when she moved on with a man—even Cade.

Gage's wellbeing was her main concern. She'd had a stepfather, and it was that same stepfather who had nearly taken from her the very virtue she easily gave to Conner.

Her brow began to sweat. In fact, it was years after her mother divorced the S.O.B. that he'd come after her. Austin picked her up and moved her to Grand Junction to hide her away, but he'd found her. It was Conner who had stepped in and took care of her. That certainly had made it easier for her to fall into his arms.

But now Cade had attached himself to Conner's son, claiming him, doting on him, making him his own. She was sure him telling her that Gage was his only family was his way of securing her heart.

Her fingers tightened around the steering wheel. Gage was hers. What if she didn't want to share him—even with his blood relative?

He was right behind her when she pulled into her driveway. There had been a moment of clarity. She didn't want to share Gage. He needed to know that.

She stepped out of the car, and it surprised her that he was standing right there. She hadn't heard him get out of the car, and how had he limped that fast? Or how long had she sat there lost in her thoughts?

There wasn't a moment to tell him what she'd thought. He wrapped his arms around her and pulled her in tight to him. A moment later, his mouth was on hers and she was lost in a sea of confusion that Cade was causing with his kiss.

It wasn't just a peck. He deepened the kiss. His tongue found hers, and when he pressed his hand against the small of her back, she was lost.

Who the hell cared who she shared her life with? Gage liked Cade, right?

She lifted up onto her toes and pressed her lips to his harder. He moved her just slightly so her back was against the car. If only she could keep Gage asleep a few more minutes, enough to carry him to his room and let him take a full nap, she could have Cade again.

"I love you, Cade." Her voice cracked as she spoke when he broke the kiss only to trail hungry ones down her neck.

He rested his forehead on hers. "I won't make you move."

"I won't make you give up your life in Wisconsin."

"We can do this. We can be a family. You, me, and Gage."

She nodded. That was what she wanted. She'd been stupid to tell him no before.

"Let me get Gage in the house and down for a nap."

Cade pulled her in tight for one more kiss. "Hurry."

Cade paced the floor as Olivia carried Gage to his room. He'd have liked to put him down, but she knew how to do it better and could get in and out. Cade would probably wake him.

There was a pent up energy surging through him now. He paced again, and this time he nicked the edge of the box with Conner's things in it with his toe.

That, too, had been eating at him. Why didn't she go through the box? Why didn't it matter?

If you had a son with someone, didn't you usually love them?

Well, that was relative, he thought. Not always was that the case.

He sat down on the couch, next to the box, and began to take out the mementos his father had tucked inside.

There was his letter jacket, his high school diploma, and a spelling bee trophy from third grade. A picture of the three of them as children in front of the tree house and a picture of Olivia and Conner at prom were in a small frame. He hadn't even realized they'd gone to prom together.

How could he have remembered any of it? He was drunk on stolen wine with Patsy in the barn at Rose Ranch. He'd been such an idiot.

At the bottom of the box there was a shoe box, and this time he was nearly paralyzed when he saw it.

"I got him down. What are..." Olivia stopped and moved next to him as he pulled it from the box.

Atop the box, his father had written Cade's name.

Cade sat back against the couch.

"He knew I'd find this."

"What's in it?" Olivia asked as she sat down next to him.

He opened the top and inside were all the papers to all the accounts that Cade would have to close out and a letter from his father.

He'd started to read it and didn't even notice that Olivia had left the room and gone into the kitchen until she came back out with two glasses of ice water. She handed him one.

"Thank you." He sipped it, unaware that his mouth had gone dry. "He knew I'd come when he died." He held the letter up. "He says he's sorry for being a bad father, bad enough that I moved away." He shook his head. That hurt because it wasn't the truth. He'd been the defiant son. "He said he came to see me play. He was there in the hospital when I was injured and that he wants me to take care of Gage because he loves him very much."

Olivia placed her hand over her mouth and batted the tears that Cade could see welling in her eyes. Tears burned his eyes too, but he'd long been trained to push them back.

"He said one of his fondest memories of our childhood was watching you and I get married under the tree with Conner officiating."

Olivia burst out in a laugh despite the tears that streaked her cheeks. "I remember that. I wore an old curtain for a veil. And we pulled flowers out of your aunt's planter, and she was going to kill us all."

"I hadn't remembered. Not until I read it."

She nodded. "You always said you'd be married to me someday."

He chuckled. "I did?"

She sat down next to him. "I know it was dumb to think a boy would keep that kind of promise, but I always hoped you would."

"Then why do you keep turning me down?"

"Because men don't mean the things they say when they're eight, and I don't want you to hate me again." She rested her hand on his knee. "You always said you'd take care of me, especially that day we hid out in the tree house when I was moving away—when you kissed me. The moment I climbed down from that tree because my stepfather was coming after us, you stopped taking care of me. I figured that was the end of us forever. Our friendship meant nothing."

"That's not true."

"But it was true. You had your life away from me. You had your friends. You had Patsy."

He let his shoulders drop. "And today I realized how stupid I had been."

She reached for his hand and interlaced their fingers. "Do you really want to take care of me forever?"

"I do."

"I have a lot of baggage."

He touched her face. "I know."

"Gage is a Carter. He should have the name."

"That would be an honor."

Olivia smiled. "If you'll have us, I'll marry you."

He'd anticipated the joy that came from her saying those words. He'd pulled her into his arms and just held her. What he hadn't known would come was the unease that settled over him. What did he know about being a husband and a father? He'd been the worst son, so why take this on?

He looked down at the box on his lap. There was something else in the bottom of it. He reached inside and pulled out a key.

Olivia grabbed it from him. "The safety deposit key."

"I have everything now, right? The papers? The key?"

She gripped the key tight in her hand. "And when you've closed out his life…"

"I'm not leaving you."

She sighed and fell into his arms. He'd spend the rest of his life proving that to her.

When Gage woke up, Cade had gone to him. Olivia didn't interfere or step in when she heard Cade gag at a dirty diaper. He'd offered. She'd accepted. She needed to let him play daddy for a few minutes. It wouldn't kill him.

Olivia walked out to the back porch and sat in the old, plastic chair. A breeze blew through the yard and the branches on the trees swayed. She closed her eyes and breathed in the bliss.

How had she gotten so mixed up with all the Carter men? She figured some people collected snow globes, others were addicted to alcohol, and she was a sucker for those blue eyes.

"You look content."

She opened her eyes and saw the two loves of her life standing in the doorway. Gage clung to Conner's teddy bear, and Cade held tight to Gage.

"I am content. I have you here. He has a silly grin on his face, and that ratty bear makes him happy. I have a home, a job, and a marriage proposal on the table. What more could a girl want?"

"Where do you want to get married?"

"In town on Monday morning at the justice of the peace."

He laughed. "Very specific."

"If I'm not specific enough, you'll leave me again. I need to wrangle you in while I can."

His smile had diminished and his eyes grew narrow. "Are you going to do this the rest of our lives? If you want to be my wife, you have to trust me."

That was true, and she was fighting it with all she had.

Olivia stood and took Gage from him. "I'm sorry. I do trust you."

"Good."

"So Monday doesn't work for you?"

Cade rubbed the back of his neck. "Not really."

She felt the disappointment creep through her. "I see."

"I need to head back to Green Bay for a few weeks and settle everything there."

Olivia moved in closer to him. "You're not staying there?" He'd said he wasn't going to make her move, but she hadn't let the thought completely settle into her mind.

"You're here. He's here. Our past is here." He smoothed her hair with his hand. "We belong here. But I have to go back and take care of everything."

"And you'll be gone a few weeks?"

"Yes. When I come back, I don't want to have to leave you again."

She wanted to cry, but she wouldn't. She'd waited all these years to marry him—again. She could wait three more weeks. "Will you marry me under the tree house?"

"Is that what you want?"

"I think it is."

"Then we will marry under our tree house." He looked at Gage. "Will you be my best man?"

"Dad," was how he replied and Olivia's knees went weak when she realized he hadn't said Dade.

Olivia had slept in his arms all weekend. Every moment they had while Gage was asleep, they made love.

One moment Cade's kisses were warm and soft. He kissed every inch of her bare skin and touched her in ways she didn't know existed. And in the dark, most quiet times of the night, there was lust that awoke in them both. Mouths were hungry. Hands grabbed and bruised tender skin, and cries were muffled—but complete ecstasy was had.

She wondered if that would be how it was from now on. She knew she'd found heaven on earth, and who would have thought it would be having Cade Carter in her life forever?

But then he was gone.

The first few days without him, once he'd returned to Green Bay, had been horrific. Gage hadn't had any night terrors the entire time Cade was with them, but the moment he'd gone back, Gage was up all night.

She assumed her lack of energy and constant state of tiredness was because Gage kept her up all night. Even if she told him Cade was coming back, he still searched for him.

Cade called every night to tell them goodnight. He emailed her pictures of the bay when there were boats sailing across. And he'd even sent her a dozen roses because it was a Thursday and she just might need something nice to look at on her desk.

These were the little things she looked forward to having in her life daily. His time away from her couldn't pass fast enough.

Parker tapped on her office door late in the afternoon just before closing. "The flowers are nice."

"Thoughtful, huh? Who would have thought?"

"I didn't get to tell you congratulations yet on your engagement."

She wasn't sure he was sincere about wanting to, but she smiled. "I almost can't believe it myself."

He stepped in further and closed the door. "I heard my sister wasn't very gracious at the festival the other day. I'm sorry."

"I don't hold it against you personally. There is no need to apologize."

"She's a nasty woman. I can't believe we came from the same set of parents."

Olivia wanted to laugh, but no matter what, Patsy was still Parker's sister.

He stood behind the chair in front of her desk and gripped the back of it. "I just really wanted to touch base with you about Cade closing out the accounts Austin has."

She nodded. "We found the safety deposit box key just the other day. So as soon as he gets back, we'll close everything out."

"Sounds good. Oh, and I heard he got a coaching job. That's going to be wonderful."

She felt the tension in her forehead as she narrowed her stare on him. "Where did you hear that?"

Parker's face lost its color, and he backed toward the door. "Around. Hey, I have a phone call I have to make. I'll catch you before you leave."

Olivia sat at her desk wondering what Parker had gotten so worked up over. If Cade had a coaching position, he'd have told her—wouldn't he?

Chapter Fifteen

Olivia waited for Cade's call, but the night grew later, and still he hadn't called.

He'd told her the night before that he'd be buried in meetings the next few days. He was a big part of the community there. He'd need to close out many things to move back to Aspen Creek.

But still, at nine o'clock at night, what kind of meeting could he possibly be in?

Olivia sent a text message, but it went unanswered. She called and left a message, but by eleven, he still hadn't called.

There was an uncomfortable tightening in her stomach, and she didn't like the uneasy feeling she was getting from it. Worry had brought on sickness. Confusion had countered with cold sweats. In the end, there was a panic sending her to the bathroom to get sick.

By midnight, she crawled into bed—exhausted and drained of emotion—and still sick.

By one in the morning, Gage was screaming.

When the sun rose, Olivia squinted against the brightness. A glance at the clock, from where she sat in the rocking chair in Gage's room with him on her shoulder, proved that the morning had come, and she'd missed it. She was already late for work.

Olivia rose, laid Gage back in his crib, and ran for the phone.

"Parker, I overslept. We had a bad night."

"Are you okay?"

"No. I'm sick, I'm tired, and now I'm late. I'll be in in an hour. Parker, I'm so sorry."

"I'll see you when you get here. Take your time."

She dropped Gage off at the daycare and profusely apologized to Michelle, explaining that her usually calm and sweet son was a monster. Michelle had laughed at her accusation, lifted Gage into her arms, and given Olivia a hug. Perhaps his day wouldn't be so bad. Hers, on the other hand, didn't seem to be getting any better.

The moment she'd walked into the bank, another chill ran through her body and her stomach uncomfortably churned. Instead of going directly into her office, she headed straight to the restroom and got sick.

Kat was quickly on her heels. "Are you okay, sweetie?"

"No," Olivia called out to her from the stall where she leaned against the cold, metal wall.

"Why are you here if you're sick?"

"Because I'm a single mother with a child in daycare. I can't miss a day of work because of the flu or some stomach bug."

She flushed the toilet and walked out of the stall. Kat stood there and watched as she washed herself up.

"I think I'm okay now. I feel much better."

Kat nodded her head. "Cade hasn't made it back yet?"

She wasn't going to stand in the restroom discussing her uncertain relationship with Cade because now she didn't know where they stood. She hadn't spoken to him. He didn't return her calls or texts, and at the very moment, she wasn't even sure she trusted his being gone.

"Cade has a lot to do in Green Bay before he can move back here."

Kat nodded again. "Then I hear you're getting married."

"That is the plan." Olivia wet a paper towel and wiped the back of her neck. "Okay, I think I'm ready to get to work. Thank you for checking on me."

"I hope you'll feel better. I know how this can drag on."

Olivia didn't quite know what she meant by that, but then again, she'd learned to not pay much attention to Kat. At some point, it all turned into idle gossip.

She left the restroom and walked quickly past Parker's office. Once in her office, she shut the door. Perhaps it would be possible to just be left alone to get her work done. There wasn't one ounce of her that felt like being social.

After an hour of making phone calls and processing loan applications, she pulled out her cell phone. There were no calls or text messages from Cade.

How could his silence break her heart so badly? She hadn't talked to him in years. Why did a few days matter?

But she couldn't help herself, and she texted him one more time. After five minutes of staring at the screen, she tucked the phone back into her purse without an answer.

Olivia worked through lunch, though that didn't do well on her ailing stomach, but she'd desperately needed the peaceful day.

It was nearly closing time when Parker opened her door and stepped in. "You've been very quiet today."

"Gage and I had a bad night. I'm sorry I was late. It won't happen again."

Parker closed the door behind him. "Olivia, I know things have been hard since Austin died. Is there anything I can do for you?"

"I've told you, everything is fine. I'm sorry…"

"Stop." He walked to her desk, but didn't stop on the other side. He walked around until he stood next to her and reached for her hand. He pulled her to her feet. "I don't care that you were late. I don't care that you've needed time off. I only care that you're okay, and I don't think you are."

"Parker, I don't understand."

"Kat told me about your condition."

She stepped back from him. "My condition?"

"I know that Cade went back to Green Bay. And I've known him as long as you have. Do you really think he's coming back here? Do you really think he'll settle here when he finds out about the baby?"

"The baby?"

Parker moved in closer and raised his hand to her cheek, gently caressing it with his thumb. "Marry me, Olivia."

"Parker, what is going on?" She reached for his hand, but she didn't move it from her cheek.

"I know you're pregnant. Kat told me. Marry me and let me take care of all of you."

This time she yanked his hand from her cheek. "You have lost your mind." She pulled open the bottom drawer of her desk and pulled out her purse. "I can't believe you listened to her. I can't believe you've come in here saying all this."

"You know how I feel about you."

"Are you kidding me? You're standing in my office saying this to me?"

"I can't seem to find a better time. Let me take care of you."

Fury pumped in her veins. "I don't need anyone to take care of me. Ever."

"I know you don't need it. I want to do this."

"Why?"

"Because I love you."

The entire world had gone crazy, and she was in the middle of it. Why would he say something like this?

"I have to go pick up Gage."

She moved past him and he reached for her, stopping her before she reached the door. "Olivia, don't leave here mad."

"You're making accusations you know nothing about. And you're being foolish."

"I may be being foolish and you might not want to marry me, but don't leave here angry at me."

She let out a breath. "I'm not angry. I don't understand your motivation."

He let his hand fall to his side. "I don't have any other motivation other than I've been crazy about you my whole life."

"Is that why you gave me this job?" She stepped closer to him. "I thought I was hired because of my skills."

"You were. Of course."

"Of course?" She narrowed her stare on him. "Did you hire me because of this silly crush you have on me?"

"No."

"Really?"

"Olivia, this has gone the wrong way. I shouldn't have…"

"Did you give me this job because of your feelings for me?"

Parker wiped his brow with the back of his hand. "No, but…"

"Oh, don't stop now."

"Austin asked my father to give you a job."

She was sure she'd stopped breathing for a moment as she stared in disbelief at Parker who fidgeted with his tie, loosening it as if he too couldn't breathe.

"I can't believe this." She adjusted her purse on her shoulder. "I guess then I will be writing up my resignation tonight."

"I won't accept it."

"I don't think you have a choice."

"Olivia, listen." He pulled the tie from his neck. "You're a huge asset to this bank. I was stupid to come in here and think that what I said was going to change your mind on things."

"Parker, I don't know what to say."

"Say you won't quit. Say you forgive me for being so stupid."

She stood there a moment and tried her best to comprehend what had just happened, but there was no way to wrap her head around it all.

"I won't quit."

"Good."

"Thank you for wanting to take care of us, but…"

"You're in love with Cade, and you're still hoping he'll come back and marry you."

She dropped her shoulders. "It may be foolish, but I'm going to keep believing it."

Parker nodded. "I admire that."

She was glad he did. With everything that had been said since Parker Woods walked into her office, she wasn't sure it was admirable to be that stupidly in love with someone. Perhaps Parker's offer wasn't so bad after all.

Chapter Sixteen

Michelle had ensured her that, though he was exhausted, Gage had had a wonderful day. Olivia was glad to hear it because her day was still on the rocks.

As they drove through town she'd seen an old Ford Bronco with Wisconsin plates. That had boiled her blood—just thinking about the fact that Cade was still in Wisconsin. She hadn't even driven by Austin's house since he'd left. Seeing it emptly would only further depress her.

She'd finally received a text from Cade: *busy, will try to call tomorrow.* That had had her nearly driving off the road reading it. But it was Parker's comments which had her wringing her hands on the steering wheel at the stop light. To find out that Austin had begged to get her a job, she didn't like that. That didn't sit well with her. But then to assume she was pregnant—that just pissed her off.

She most certainly wasn't pregnant. She took precautions against things like that, even though she hadn't been with anyone else in nearly two years. But...

The light turned green, and the car behind her honked.

Olivia drove toward the house, but the thought that *what if Kat was right* nagged at her. Was that why she was sick? Did she really get pregnant again?

There were millions of women in the world who couldn't get pregnant, and she could get pregnant each time she had *protected* sex with a man? What good was a birth control pill anyway?

The cold sweat was back. She looked in the back seat, and Gage had fallen asleep. A glance at the clock told her it was already nearing six. Certainly she wasn't going to buy a pregnancy test in town—even though it was going to be negative. She'd have to drive over the hill to Aspen Hills to buy it.

It would put her mind at ease, and when it was negative perhaps she'd go to the doctor and find out why she didn't feel good, though she assumed it was all the stress Cade was putting her under.

She quickly turned left and headed out of town.

Cade hated assembling furniture as much as he hated moving. He'd accepted his coaching position, and he was glad Ashley had given him that phone call. He'd been right. It was the coaching position of a lifetime, and he'd never have passed it up. Only now he was settling into a house he never thought he'd live in, assembling furniture he'd had to buy, and smelling paint fumes, which were making him sick. But it would all be worth it.

Though when he'd realized that Olivia had called and paged him as many times as she had, he figured he'd better give her a little something before she completely hated him all over again. The text was short and simple. He'd call her soon, just not yet.

As he stood up to look at the night stand he'd assembled, his phone rang again. This time it was Ashley.

"You settled in?"

Cade wiped the back of his neck with his hand. "Almost. How come I didn't just bring the furniture out of that house?"

"Because you sold this to me with everything in it."

Cade laughed. "Right."

"And I have to tell you, I'm loving that car!" He was nearly singing. "You wouldn't believe how fast I got it going the other day."

Cade shook his head. "Don't kill yourself. I wouldn't forgive myself."

"I promise. After all, I'll be heading out there soon to see you get married." Ashley coughed in the phone. "I can't believe I said that aloud. Cade Carter—a married man with a kid. Who would have ever guessed?"

"Certainly not me." He took the wrench out of his pocket and tightened another bolt. "I thought my cover was blown today. She was driving through town when I passed her."

"You're really an idiot, aren't you? Why would you want to be there and not tell her?"

"Because I want to surprise her. You should see my old room. Gage is going to love it."

"Well, I think that injury scrambled your brains, but I have to say, I don't think I've ever seen you happier. I'll see you next week."

Cade turned off the phone and slid it back in his pocket. She was going to love him even more when she found out he'd been finishing up his father's house so they could live there as a family after their surprise wedding under the tree.

Olivia sat on her bed and tried to breathe. It wasn't going very well. Gage had been asleep for hours. He was very tired, and she'd been sitting there nearly as long.

What was she going to do now?

She stared at the pregnancy test as if it were going to change its mind. She was pregnant with Cade Carter's baby.

Before she'd taken the test, she'd called him and there was no answer. She'd sent him two more text messages to call her, but he hadn't. It was clear in her mind that he'd forgotten all about her, and now she was pregnant, again, with another Carter child.

At least when she ran to the bathroom this time, she knew why she was sick.

He didn't love her. He didn't want them. Only now, there were more of them.

She cleaned herself up and stared at the reflection in the mirror. She'd be damned if he'd do this to her. He'd want the baby. He wasn't Conner. Cade understood what it meant to be a good parent. She'd seen him with Gage. He loved him.

Well, if he wasn't going to return her text messages or phone calls, there was only one thing to do.

Olivia headed back to her bedroom, took out her suitcase, and started to pack. She and Gage were going on a road trip. How could he turn her away if she was standing on his front porch?

Chapter Seventeen

Cade stood in the kitchen and looked around. In one week, the house had been transformed. New carpet, new furniture, and he had a whole new outlook on life.

Next week he'd have the rest of Conner's old house taken out, but for now, he was enjoying the bliss that was his new life.

He'd never expected the call from Coach Cal offering him the measly job of high school football coach right there in Aspen Creek, but it had been the right job at the right time. He and Olivia would be very happy in their little town, in the only house either of them had ever called home.

Cade poured out the last bit of his coffee into the new sink and even loaded the mug into the new dishwasher. The call from his lawyer had come in the night before, and he'd drawn up all the necessary papers to adopt Gage and give him that Carter name he deserved.

Everything felt just right.

Now all he had to do was take the key to the safety deposit box to the bank, and if he'd calculated right, Olivia should be working.

Cade took in a deep breath and let it out slow. Life couldn't be any more perfect.

Downtown Aspen Creek was still quiet when Cade rolled through Main Street. He'd stopped by Mindy Field's and grabbed a fancy coffee for Olivia and a muffin. He thought the cran-orange one was the one she'd ordered.

His next stop was the grocery store where he picked up a bouquet of flowers.

He didn't see her car when he pulled into the parking lot of the bank. Perhaps he'd just not seen it on the other side of the building.

Cade stepped out of the Bronco. Who would have thought he'd enjoy having it more than the Porsche. But a new car, with room for Gage, was certainly in his future. Perhaps a new car for Olivia, too. Something he could trust in the snow.

The bank was empty except for Parker and Kat, who both lifted their heads when he walked through the door with his arms loaded down with flowers, coffee, and muffins.

"Cade, I didn't know you were in town." Parker walked toward him.

"Yeah." He looked around. "Isn't Olivia working today?"

Parker and Kat exchanged looks. "She called me at ten o'clock last night and said she needed a few days off. She left this morning for Wisconsin."

"She what?" He had to focus and not drop everything in his arms. "Why?" He sounded stupid, but he could tell he was completely left out of the loop.

Kat had walked out to the lobby and was standing next to Parker. "Oh, Cade, look at you bearing gifts. Caffeine isn't good for her."

"I beg your pardon."

"Expectant mothers shouldn't drink things like that. It's not good for the baby."

Cade shifted his eyes back to Parker.

Parker took a step back. "Kat, you don't know that."

"Hmmm." She moved closer to Cade. "Give me those and let me put them in some water. Parker, take Mr. Carter into your office and conduct business in there. I see Mrs.

Abilene, and she doesn't need a scene in the lobby of the bank."

Carter didn't know what to think about the crazy conversation Kat seemed to be holding with herself, but he followed a very nervous Parker into his office and sat in front of his desk as Parker closed the door.

"Cade, I'm sorry about that. Kat seems to have…"

"Olivia is pregnant?"

Parker let out a long breath and it was pissing Cade off. What did he already know that Cade didn't? The worst images were popping into his head. Maybe she was pregnant, and maybe the baby was Parker's. Then again, if he knew about it, why would Olivia have gone to Wisconsin?

Parker sat down behind his desk. "Kat decided that because Olivia hadn't been feeling well, she must be pregnant."

"So, she's not?"

Parker only shrugged. "I don't know. I got a little worked up over it and made a huge scene and…"

Cade was on his feet, and he couldn't help but notice how pathetic Parker looked literally cowering behind his desk. Cade backed down and sat in the chair.

"What kind of scene?"

Parker wiped his hand across his forehead. "I asked her to marry me."

"You what?" He was back up and out of his chair again.

Parker stood. "Cade, I have cared about her as long as you have. It just always seemed as if I was the only one who remembered that she needed to be taken care of. You and Patsy were always causing her so much pain."

"And you think it will always be that way?"

"C'mon, be realistic."

At that moment he could have put Parker through a wall, but then again, throwing Buck into the jukebox had only made him look the part of the stupid bully he'd obviously been known for.

Cade tried to calm down. He set the coffee and the muffin on Parker's desk. "I'm not going to back down this time. I love her, and I hope you can respect that." It sounded mature enough when he said it.

"I know. She wasn't happy with me for proposing. She even threatened to resign."

"She quit her job?"

"No, I asked her not to. But when she found out your dad had arranged with my father for her to have a job, she was furious."

Cade sunk back in his chair. "He arranged the job?"

"Your dad did a lot of things for her after Gage was born. You can imagine Kat's tongue wagging then."

Cade fisted his hands tightly. "She didn't have an affair with my father."

"I know that. She told me."

Cade took his father's will and the paperwork Olivia had needed out of his pocket and set it on Parker's desk. "My father left everything in his accounts to Gage. Here is his will." He pushed it toward him. "I want to sign it all over to him."

"We can do that."

He reached into his front pocket and pulled out the safety deposit box key and set it on the desk, too. "He left me the contents of the box. Do you suppose I could see it?"

"Yes." Parker pulled papers out from the drawer of his desk. "We have some paperwork to do first."

"Great."

At least he'd have the accounts arranged before Olivia came back.

Damn, he needed to stop her.

Olivia had called Parker as she pulled out onto the highway last night. Once she'd recovered from the shock that she was pregnant, she'd packed, put Gage in the car, and drove way. She was exhausted.

There had been a small nest egg she'd kept. She'd always hoped to pay Austin back with it, but under the circumstances, she thought using it to purchase an airline ticket would be acceptable. She had to get to Cade and tell him about the baby.

At this point, she wasn't sure what he'd do, and she didn't care. But he had the means to take care of his baby, and he'd said he'd take care of Gage since he was the only relative he had left. Olivia thought it was time Cade Carter take care of something in his life.

The flight was long. Gage didn't understand what was going on, and he was restless throughout the entire flight.

She could only hope that when she made it to Green Bay the taxi ride to his house wouldn't take up the rest of her funds, but she couldn't be sure. She'd looked up the address Austin had had for Cade. God, what if he didn't live there anymore?

Olivia gave the taxi driver the address. She took in the scenery as they headed toward Cade's house.

Wisconsin was beautiful.

Oh, was she holding him back by asking him to move back to Aspen Creek?

The moment Gage yelled "Dade," she turned with a jerk. Bigger than life, there a picture of him on a billboard.

He still belonged to this community.

Her heart squeezed in her chest. None of this was going to work unless she moved. Gage's eyes were wide as he watched the huge body of water outside the window. Even Olivia couldn't believe that was just a lake.

When the driver pulled up to the house, there was a gate at the street with a speaker box. He pulled up far enough so she could press the button.

"He-loo." It was a woman's voice on the other end, and her English was extremely broken.

"I am here to see Cade Carter."

"You have appointment?"

Olivia laughed. This certainly wasn't expected. He was more well off than she'd even assumed.

"No, I don't have an appointment. I am his fiancée."

For a moment, there was silence. "You his what?"

"His fiancée."

"Miser Carter not here. You want to see Ashley?"

There was a knot in her throat. "Pardon me?"

"Ashley live here. You talk to Ashley."

The tears stung her eyes. Her stomach tightened. The weight of her crashing world was heavy on her shoulders.

"No, I don't want to talk to Ashley."

The tears fell. She couldn't stop them. The entire trip had been a mistake. "Take us back to the airport please," she told the driver.

How was she going to take care of two children on her own?

And why hadn't she seen this coming? The bastard already lived with another woman.

Chapter Eighteen

Parker and Cade had signed everything over to Gage and closed out anything else. He hadn't realized how long his father had done business in that town.

"I'll go get the box for you," Parker said just as Cade's phone rang.

He looked at it. It was Ashley. Thank God.

"Rumor has it my girl is headed your way. I can't get a hold of her."

"Cade, shut the hell up. She's been here."

"Listen, this isn't how I wanted this to go, but keep her there. Make her comfortable. I'll get the next flight out."

"Damn it, Cade. I don't have her, you idiot. She came in a cab. Consuela told her you weren't here."

Cade let out a groan. "She just left."

"You bet she did. As soon as Consuela told her you were gone and Ashley lived there. She could talk to Ashley."

Cade shook his head. At first, Ashley wasn't even making sense. What did it matter if... "Oh, dear Lord! She thinks I left to go back to Green Bay to some woman."

"That's what I'd be thinking. See, my mama was causing trouble way back when."

"And I haven't talked to her all week. I was hiding, trying to get everything together."

"I've said it before. I'm saying it again. You're an idiot."

"I'm feeling it."

Parker walked through the door with the box in his hand and set it on the desk.

Cade turned to the side. "Dude, get here on the next flight. We're going to do this tomorrow."

Ashley groaned. "At some point, I assume you're going to let me lounge in peace in my new house with my new car."

"Sure, but until then, get here."

"Wouldn't miss it for the world."

Cade ended the call and turned back to the desk. Parker stood there. "You're welcome to stay in here and go through this."

He looked at the box. This was all that was left minus the keepsakes Cade had stored in the basement.

"You don't have to go," he said, almost as if he didn't want to be left alone with his father.

Parker nodded and took his seat.

There wasn't much in the box. A few titles to cars, ones he didn't even think were around anymore. Maybe his father had forgotten about the box. He'd find out in time. There was the title to the house, which would be needed.

Cade pulled out a long box and opened it.

He heard Parker take a deep breath. "Conner's Purple Heart."

Cade looked up at him.

"Your dad showed it to me before he put it in the box. He thought it would be safe in there after Conner died. He wasn't even sure his sister knew about it."

"Olivia told me what happened."

"I can't imagine what he saw. It's too bad his life wasn't different from the start. He was a fantastic man. Things just turned."

Cade nodded his head. He wished he could have known the man Conner had become. He'd keep the medal safe for Gage. That would be something honorable to know about your father. This was his chance to make Conner Carter bigger than life, and he was going to do just that.

There was one more box left in the safety deposit box, and this one was a ring box.

He pulled it out and hesitantly opened it.

Inside was a diamond solitaire. He'd have guessed an engagement ring. Had his father planned to give that to Olivia? Had Conner?

He closed the box and continued with the few items left.

There were more receipts for items that Cade couldn't identify and an old silver dollar. He laughed at the random things left in the box. At the bottom was an envelope of pictures.

They were black and white and of his father at a much younger age. He saw the resemblance now. He certainly was his father's child.

He flipped to the next picture and froze. It was the first time he'd seen his mother's face since she'd left them. Honestly, he didn't remember her at all. She could have walked up to him on the street, and he wouldn't have known her. But to see her, standing next to his father, he remembered her.

The picture after that was of his parents standing over their wedding cake. The ring in the box had been his mother's.

There was a pang in his heart. He wanted Olivia to have the ring. Not because his mother didn't care about it, but it symbolized everything else. Olivia knew his mother couldn't have stayed in Aspen Creek. Certainly he'd inherited her wanderlust. But it symbolized the sacrifice his father made to stay in the town to raise him. And if it hadn't been for that, he'd never have met Olivia.

It was also something his father picked out for the woman he loved. Likewise, he knew his father loved Olivia. And, if he hadn't been so stubborn, he probably would have married her and given Gage a name, no matter what people thought.

Would she understand the sentiment of him giving her a ring his father had purchased? It would be as though it were from both of them.

That was if she would ever speak to him again.

Ashley had better get to Aspen Creek as fast as he could before Cade ruined everything.

Olivia did everything she could to make Gage comfortable while they waited for a seat on a flight back to Denver. She only wished she could make herself more comfortable.

She'd known heartbreak before. The first time she'd ever felt it was sitting in that damn tree house in Cade's back yard when her stepfather pulled her from the tree. Over the years, her heart had ached for every Carter man she'd known. But this hurt the worst. He'd lied to her from the very start and now she carried his child.

How could she have been so foolish to have gone to bed with him? Gage would be devastated in time and angry when he grew to understand.

If Cade lied about this, he certainly wouldn't be the best role model for a child. She'd be doing this alone—again.

The flight was long and bumpy. Denver was hot and dry. Of course, there was traffic the entire way back to Aspen Creek. The drive was already long enough without it. Add that to constant breaks for food for Gage and rest for her, it had taken nearly eight hours to make a four hour trip. She didn't arrive home until ten-thirty that night.

The house was dark and looked as sad as she felt. She tucked Gage into bed and headed for the shower. Tomorrow was Monday morning, and even though she'd informed Parker she wouldn't be there, she had no intentions of taking one more day off of work. She was going to need to save every cent she could get her hands on.

The look on Parker's face let her know he certainly hadn't expected her. He followed her into her office and shut the door.

"You said you'd be gone all week."

She slammed the drawer after putting her purse in it and snapped her head up to look at him. "Change of plans. So are you going to fire me for coming into work?"

"What? No." He moved toward her and she backed away. That stopped him. "I just thought…"

"I don't care what anyone has thought. I'm back. I'm not going anywhere so let me get to work."

Their conversation was interrupted by a knock at the door, and Kat opening it before she was invited in.

"You have someone here to see you."

"I don't want to see…"

The man behind Kat walked straight in.

He had to have been the tallest man Olivia had ever seen, and Parker's expression teetered on excitement and annoyance. He slid his sunglasses off his face and put them on the back of his neck, just as Cade would do. That only revealed the most stunning set of blue eyes Olivia had ever seen. The sharp contrast with his caramel skin made her speechless.

"Ms. Baker?"

"That's me." Her voice cracked as he walked toward her with an enormous bouquet of red roses cradled in his arm.

He held out his free hand for her to shake. "Ashley Wilkie."

She took the man's hand and noticed that when he'd said his name both Parker's and Kat's eyes shot wide open. "Mr. Wilkie, it's nice to meet you."

"These are for you." He handed her the bouquet.

"Thank you, but…"

He held up his hand. "I also have this for you." He handed her an envelope with a card inside.

It was hard to take her eyes off the man standing before her to open the envelope. When she did, she found an invitation.

Your presence is requested
at the marriage of
Olivia Baker and Cade Carter
this afternoon at 5PM
Under the Tree House

Olivia's mouth had fallen open as she looked up at the man ginning before her.

He cleared his throat. "I would have been the Ashley you heard about in Green Bay. My mother had a funny sense of humor."

"Ashley?" She let it settle in her mind. "You're Ashley?"

"Yes, ma'am. Mr. Carter has been here for the past week with his new coaching job at the high school and settling in so that he could marry you."

"Cade was here?"

Parker stepped forward. "He came in yesterday to see you. He didn't know you'd left for Wisconsin."

"So, he isn't married or doesn't have some girlfriend?"

Ashley shook his head. "No, ma'am. He's got it bad for you, and trust me, I've lived around the man for a long time. I've never seen him quite like this."

Olivia pressed her fingers to her lips. "He still wants to marry me?"

"Under the tree at five."

She looked at Parker.

"You weren't scheduled this week. Perhaps you should go home."

At that moment, Michelle walked into her office with Gage on her hip. He jumped down and raced to her.

Olivia scooped him into her arms and looked back at Michelle.

Michelle shrugged her shoulders. "I got a call from Cade that said I needed to get Gage to your office right away and then follow you home to help you."

Tears were stinging her eyes, but they wouldn't fall. They were happy tears, and she'd rather keep the stupid grin on her face that she could feel tugging at her cheeks.

"I think you need to help me get dressed."

Michelle was obviously as clueless as the rest of them—all except for Ashley Wilkie, whom she found out later from Michelle was some big time football hero, almost as famous as Cade Carter.

Chapter Nineteen

Michelle had followed her home and helped her take Gage from the car. Olivia wasn't sure why she was surprised when she walked through the front door and found, draped on the chair, a white dress and a new pair of shoes.

The tears fell then as Michelle walked in behind her.

"This has got to be the sweetest thing I have ever seen."

Olivia shook her trembling hands. "He meant it. He meant it all along. God, he promised me he'd marry me when he was six. And a few more times over the years, but I didn't think it would ever happen."

She walked to the chair and picked up the dress. Under the dress was a tuxedo Gage's size. The tears streamed full force now.

As she picked it up to show it to him, she noticed legal papers beneath it. She handed Michelle the tuxedo. On the papers, which were drafted by an attorney in Wisconsin, there was a yellow sticky note. *This is what I want from you as my wedding gift.*

Michelle walked up beside her. "What is it?"

"Adoption papers. He wants to adopt Gage."

Cade paced beneath the old tree house in the back yard of his father's house. A drape of white netting had been hung from the branches and a few folding chairs from the local Christian church had been lined up in the back yard. There wouldn't be many people at their wedding, but those who were there were the ones who mattered.

Who would have thought that he'd almost lost everything when he tried to give her the perfect day.

He'd seen Michelle walk out of the house holding Gage's hand. That meant Olivia had arrived.

Gage let go of Michelle's hand and ran to Cade. He lifted him into his arms and gave him the biggest squeeze a man could give a child. *His* child.

Ashley rested his hand on Cade's shoulder. "I thought I witnessed history that day on that field, but I think I'm about to witness it again."

"I've waited my whole life for this."

The back door opened to the house, and he saw her. The most beautiful vision he'd ever seen.

The thudding in his chest went deeper than it did that day when he had stood in the same spot with Conner to his side. They'd both been breathless when she walked toward them with her curtain-draped head. Now, here she was— the most beautiful woman he'd ever known, walking toward him in the dress he'd picked out for her—along with Conner's son.

She'd been crying, but the smile let him know they were tears of joy.

"You came."

Olivia let out a deep breath. "You're not living with some woman named Ashley."

They both chuckled, and he reached his hand to her cheek. "I've never seen anyone so beautiful in my entire life."

"Thank you." She turned to Michelle, and she handed her the papers Cade had left for her. "These are for you."

He looked down at them as everyone watched them. The minister to his side waited patiently.

He turned to the page where she was to sign them and noticed that she had. Marriage was one thing, but to become a father—that moment filled him with a love and passion that even Olivia couldn't have brought out in him.

"He's our son now."

"You've made me the happiest man in the world. Do you know that?"

"I don't think I have yet." She moved in closer to them and wrapped her arms around both Cade and Gage. "My gift to you is my son, whom I love and I know you do, too. But I have another gift for you. A child of your own."

The thudding that had been in his chest moved to his throat, and he could feel the blood drain from his face. "A child of my own?"

"Yes."

"You're…"

She smiled wide. "Yes."

He scrubbed his hand over his face and let it all sink in. "We're a family again."

Olivia nodded. "And I saw what you did to the house. It looks like you plan to make a home right here were home always was."

"That was the plan."

"I don't think you could make me any happier, Cade Carter."

"Let me try." He turned to Ashley and motioned to the pocket in his suit. Ashley handed him the ring he held. "This was in my father's safety deposit box." He slid the ring on her finger. "If he hadn't given up everything to settle here and raise me, I wouldn't have you. If he wouldn't have given Conner a home, we wouldn't have Gage. If he wouldn't have put everything right in place, I wouldn't have come to the funeral at all. He made sure we found each other. He made sure we were together just as we were supposed to do."

"I knew I loved that old man."

"I did too. I'd just forgotten how much."

Olivia rested her head on Cade's shoulder. "I want to name the baby Austin, even if she's a girl."

"I think that would be wonderful."

"I'm so happy that I'm marrying you right here under our tree so that our first kiss as husband and wife will be in the same place where we shared our first kiss."

Cade kissed the top of Gage's head and then the top of Olivia's. "Then let's get married."

Meet the Author

Bernadette Marie has been an avid writer since the early age of 13, when she'd fill notebook after notebook with stories that she'd share with her friends. Her journey into novel writing started the summer before eighth grade when her father gave her an old typewriter. At all times of the day and night you would find her on the back porch penning her first work, which she would continue to write for the next 22 years.

In 2007—after marriage, filling her chronic entrepreneurial needs, and having five children—Bernadette began to write seriously with the goal of being published. That year she wrote 12 books. In 2009 she was contracted for her first trilogy and the published author was born. In 2011 she (being the entrepreneur that she is) opened her own publishing house, 5 Prince Publishing, and has released her own contemporary titles. She also quickly began the process of taking on other authors in other genres.

In 2012 Bernadette Marie began to find herself on the bestsellers lists of iTunes, Amazon, and Barnes and Noble to name a few. Her office wall is lined with colorful PostIt notes with the titles of books she will be releasing in the very near future, with hope that they too will grace the bestsellers lists.

Bernadette spends most of her free time driving her kids to their many events—usually hockey. She is also an accomplished martial artist with a second degree black belt in Tang Soo Do. An avid reader, she enjoys contemporary romances with humor and happily ever afters.